DEVIL'S NIGHT

STEFON MEARS

Thousand Faces Publishing

Also by Stefon Mears

Published by Thousand Faces Publishing, Portland, Oregon

http://1kfaces.com

Copyright © 2019 by Stefon Mears

Front cover image © Andreykuzmin | Dreamstime.com

ISBN: 978-1-948490-00-9

PROLOGUE

For once, it looked as though Long Pine High was fucked up in Bishop's favor.

Gods knew they owed him one.

Sophomore year? They'd canceled the music department, just when he was getting good at classical guitar. Sure, he'd kept at the guitar on his own, but that wasn't the point.

Just *eliminating* the music department? That was some serious bullshit.

The same kind of bullshit they pulled just before junior year. When somebody on the PTA got a bug up their butt about the school mascot.

As though anyone ever went Satanist over a high school mascot.

So instead of the Long Pine Green Devils, they became the Long Pine Cormorants. Which made about as much sense, far as Bishop was concerned. Weren't any more cormorants hanging around a Bay Area suburb than there were green devils.

But Bishop's best friend, Ans, did all the art for the school promotions. Blessing and curse of being so good at it.

Ans drew some *kickass* green devils. But drawing stupid birds bored him, so Bishop had to listen to him complain every time a new project came his way.

Least Bishop could do, though. Ans had listened with nothing but sympathy while Bishop bitched about losing the music department.

This time, though. Halloween. This was different.

This time, old Principal Null may have finally gotten one right.

This year, Halloween fell on a Saturday. Most natural thing in the world — the thing any school with a lick of sense would have done — would have been to hold the Halloween Dance on Halloween itself.

That would have been perfect, in its own way.

Faye, Bishop's girlfriend of two years, she *loved* to dance. Just like Ans' girl, Jewel. The dances always started around seven, and Steve Jenkins' annual Halloween bash never really started before nine or ten.

Bishop and Ans could have danced 'til Faye and Jewel were all breathless and happy. Perfect mood to party for a couple of hours at Steve's place before splitting off into couples and rounding out the night with little private parties of their own.

Would have been a *fine* evening all around.

But the school had a football game slated for Saturday. And no way no how would they move a football game for a dance.

Sure. Logic would have said they should hold the game and *then* the dance. But as Ans always joked, the only "logic" in Long Pine High School involved anagrams.

Turned out the school couldn't hold a dance and a game on the same night. Some kind of issue there with insurance, or overtime, or...

Truth was, Bishop tuned out during Mr. Michelson's explanation, back during first period Calculus that morning.

He got the gist of it. The part that *mattered*.

And what mattered was that the dance was Friday night. Not Saturday night.

And that, well, that might work out even better.

Bishop didn't care much about football, and neither did Ans. But

Faye and Jewel were both on the cheer squad — they'd joined up sophomore year when Faye's younger sister Gemma made the football team as a place kicker — so they never missed a game.

And while cheering wasn't quite as good as dancing, when it came to Faye and Jewel getting breathless and happy, it came in a pretty close second. By the time the game was over, they'd be eager to change into their costumes and head out to Steve's party.

So Halloween night projected to be pretty darn good.

And as for the night before, it might be even better.

Bishop and Ans had been friends since fifth grade, when Ans moved out here from Detroit. In Detroit, the night before Halloween was known as Devil's Night, and got famous because people liked to set fire to abandoned houses on that night.

Ans wasn't a firebug, but when he moved out here, he couldn't believe Long Pine City didn't do *anything* for Devil's Night.

So naturally, Ans had wanted to start a little Devil's Night tradition of his own. But he didn't have any good ideas.

Bishop had suggested finding a haunted kind of place, and telling ghost stories. Ans loved it.

And for years, the two of them had done just that. Cemeteries, empty parks, all kinds of places within reach of their bikes. They'd huddle together with flashlights and try to scare the hell out of each other.

They didn't sleep much those nights, but they had a good time.

Then Bishop and Ans had gotten old enough to start inviting girls to join in their little tradition. Some went for it. Some didn't.

The ones that didn't, well, they didn't tend to stick around very long.

Faye and Jewel got into it. Even brought stories of their own to tell, which was just proof of how awesome they were.

And now, for the first time since junior high, Devil's Night fell on a *Friday*.

They could dance it up for a couple of hours in the gym. Then they could head off to a nice secluded spot — Ans said he'd found the perfect place for this year — jazz each other up even more with some ghost stories. Keep at it 'til their hearts were pounding, and they were clinging to each other...

And not one of them had to be home before *three*. Benefit of being seniors.

Oh, yes. Long Pine High might have been pretty fucked up, but this time that might actually work out in Bishop's favor.

He couldn't wait.

1

———

OCTOBER 30TH, JUST BEFORE 3:15 PM.

AUTO SHOP — BISHOP'S BEST FRIEND AND HIS WORST ENEMY.

Four years of Auto Shop had saved Bishop more money in car expenses than he could track.

That class was the reason he'd gotten away with paying fifty bucks for a trashed relic of a Dodge Charger from the mid-70s. He'd bought that car as a freshman, and spent two years rebuilding it before he was even legally old enough to fire it up.

By senior year, the Charger wasn't looking pristine or anything, but it did look pretty decent. Sure, half the parts had the mismatched paint jobs of their original vehicles, but the rust was gone, the body was in good shape, and the upholstery even matched now.

Best of all, the Charger purred like jungle cat.

Bishop loved that image. Deep down, he wanted to call his sweet ride the Panther.

Unfortunately, Ans had christened it the Frankencharger back in Sophomore year, and the name stuck.

At least Ans was talking about helping with the paint job, around graduation. Something that would fit the Frankencharger theme. And with Ans planning the look, the result might be cooler than any cat theme could hope to be.

But today was one of those days when Auto Shop was Bishop's worst enemy.

The class was only available during the seventh period slot — the last of the day — which meant that a good hour after pretty much every other senior was free and clear for Halloween weekend, Bishop was stuck in here, checking brake pads that didn't need checking, and trying to get that smell out of the air conditioner.

Something had gotten into the system on that trip to Santa Cruz last month, and the car still smelled like a tide pool every time Bishop turned on the fan.

Couldn't focus on that though. Didn't want to take apart the dashboard and get caught up in tracking down odors. Not today. It was all he could do to look busy enough to not get hassled by Mr. Stevenson.

Mr. Stevenson taught this class as a kind of retirement job after some forty years of work at different garages. These days, he could let his gray hair and beard grow long — his hair was almost as long as Bishop's, which made the old man smile — and his belly "nice and round" as Mr. Stevenson described it.

Bishop thought Mr. Stevenson looked like a Hell's Angels version of Santa Claus.

And woe betide those students who thought they'd slack off in his class. Mr. Stevenson had the most creative approach to punishments. Auto Shop was full of dirty, disgusting jobs that Mr. Stevenson kept ready for anyone he caught letting more than their motor idle.

Even on a day like today, those hawk eyes of his kept darting. It was driving Bishop crazy, and the school clock seemed to go slower and slower and...

Finally the bell rang. The sweetest music.

Bishop was sending texts before he even fired up his car.

Free! (sent to Ans, Faye and Jewel)

Finally! (from Faye, who didn't have much right to complain.

Cheerleading practice was also a seventh period activity, though they didn't meet every day.)

Smiling emoji from Jewel, and a thumbs-up from Ans.

"Stay safe out there!" Mr. Stevenson called as his students filed or drove out of his huge garage, as he did at the end of every class.

Bishop hopped behind the wheel. The solid thump of his door closing, the sound of completion.

He cranked the key. The Frankencharger growled to life, accompanied by Metallica's cover of "Am I Evil."

Bishop winked at himself in the rearview mirror, and peeled out.

The sad part of peeling out of Auto Shop is that it was anticlimactic. A joyous moment like that should have led to rapid use of the oak gear shift knob, and racing for a freeway or something. Maybe just hitting three yellow lights along the way. Really letting the Charger off its school-day leash.

But it was not to be. Not here.

The school driveway let out onto a side street, with a speed limit of twenty, and a cop sitting there every day. *Almost* hidden behind a tall hedge. Just waiting to give Bishop a ticket.

All right, maybe the mustached jerk didn't care who he ticketed, but he'd nailed Bishop three times, and always did it with this evil smile. Last time was for twenty-three miles per hour.

Twenty-three.

Bishop refused to even learn the cop's name, out of a small, petty sort of revenge. The better revenge was what Bishop was getting right now.

Bishop saw the jerk look up at the sound of Frankencharger's roar. Guy was already firing up his bike. Ready to hit the siren. Ready to catch Bishop for number four.

But Bishop had a plan. Tested it in late night parking lots, just to make sure.

By the time his speedometer passed fifteen, Bishop's foot was already off the gas. The needle reached twenty, but didn't even shrug a hair across the line.

Twenty miles-per-hour exactly, all the way up two blocks of

boring suburbia to the first stop sign. Nothing but perfectly mown lawns and happy little houses all around him. The kind with front yard tire swings hanging from the occasional elm tree, and the goofiest kind of store bought Halloween decorations.

A cavalcade of kitsch.

But when Bishop hit that stop sign, he smiled into his rearview mirror. The jerk cop was sitting *way* back there. Hadn't budged an inch from his "hiding" spot. But from the tilt of his helmet, he was still watching Bishop.

Bishop turned the corner and punched it.

He liked to think that cop heard the Frankencharger's roar, but sat there impotent, too far away to do anything about it.

Or maybe he fired up his bike. Gave chase. But Bishop was already turning again at the next block and killing his speed. Even if the jerk caught up to him, Bishop wouldn't be doing anything wrong.

Heh.

Home was only another ten blocks anyway. Hardly worth the effort of driving at all, except for three key things.

First, taunting the cop. Of course. Jerk was asking for it. Hassling high school students like that. If he wanted to catch real speeders, he should have been down near the office parks that let out onto Highway 280. Those guys hit freeway speeds on city streets.

Second reason, the joy of awesome music pounding in his ears from the best car stereo Bishop could afford.

Most important of all, the sweet freedom of *driving*.

Yeah. These were things worth Auto Shop, worth staying every day through seventh period, even worth dealing with that jerk cop. Especially key number three.

Nothing was better than freedom.

When the ping came, Ans was almost finished with his sketch. One of his big sketchbooks, of course. Eighteen by eleven inches. Rough paper. Best to start new projects with.

He only worked with medium pencils when doing his first drafts. Not because they were best for what he was doing. No, it was because he *thought* best in medium pencil. A habit picked up when he was a kid, before he learned how many options a proper drawing kit would give him.

This sketch was a haunted house. Victorian. Dark sky. Overgrown grass with weeds. Huge oak in the yard with the tattered remnants of an old noose, only just visible as it danced in the wind.

Smears of clouds in the night sky, barely hiding the half-moon.

Everyone always thought of full moons as the scariest kind of moon. Ans preferred the half-moon. Like a guillotine hanging in the sky. Or the headsman's axe, ready to come down.

The house itself, a little decrepit, but not too much. Just implications here and there. Boards on the porch, the shutters on the windows. Those were the kinds of things suggesting an inner rot in the house. Disrepair. Danger.

And in the attic window, a shadow.

Ans didn't even know what it was a shadow of. Sometime between the initial sketch and the time he started working on his tablet, he'd make more decisions. Or, rather, the decisions would let him know what they were.

That was how drawing always felt to Ans, when it was good. Like he wasn't making any decisions at all. He was just looking in on some other universe, and drawing what he saw there.

But the ping came, which meant it was finally a quarter past three, and Bish was done with Auto Shop.

Ans fired back a quick thumbs-up emoji, and shook himself. Reminded himself where he was.

The front bench seat of his ancient Caddy. Stereo didn't work, the interior smelled like French fries all the time, and despite Bishop's best efforts, it still leaked oil at a slow, steady rate. But it was roomy and comfortable. Plus, it always managed to pass smog, had a trunk that could hide a full-grown heifer, and could get him anywhere he needed to go.

Not to mention, it had that big, big back seat.

Oh, the fun Ans and Jewel had had in that back seat.

Might be where they'd have some of their fun tonight. After the dance, and the Devil's Night stories.

Eight years out here from Detroit, and Ans still had trouble believing sometimes that nobody in the Bay Area did anything for Devil's Night. They didn't have to start fires or anything, but it just seemed like a missed opportunity for more Halloween fun.

Like the way some families make as big a deal out of Christmas Eve as they do about Christmas.

Ah, well.

Ans stretched and closed his sketchpad. Slipped it into his big, blue backpack. Zipped the backpack closed, and held it up to the afternoon sun.

He looked over the array of hand-drawn band logos and obscure occult symbols he'd dug out of old books.

He hadn't added the Misfits yet, and that was wrong. Could copy it right off the Fiend Club shirt he was wearing. Ought to be a good spot for the skull and band name right up near the handle...

Ans shook himself again. No time to play with Sharpies now. Bish was out of class, which meant he'd be here in a minute or two, unless he got stopped by the jerk cop again.

Nah. Not today. Bish wouldn't chance anything ruining today.

Ans slung his backpack over his shoulder as he got out of his car. Stretched a little more, and glanced at the sky. Still clear, despite the way the wind had picked up. Sometimes it rained around Halloween, but it didn't look like this year.

Good. No sense in getting their costumes wet.

Well, more importantly, no sense in getting the *girls'* costumes wet. That might spoil the night's fun faster than anything.

Fallen maple leaves rustled their way up the block. Every freaking house on this block — Bishop's included — had two maple trees out by the curb. Place didn't even have a homeowner's association, so Ans couldn't imagine how it had worked out that way. And yet it had.

Bishop's house started life as a one-story place, but about three years ago, his parents had put on a second floor. Not to mention a hot tub and a lap pool out back.

York Dentistry must have been doing well. Not that Ans and Bishop ever talked about money. Well, their parents' money, anyway. The lamentable state of their own funds was a common enough thread of conversation.

Ans cocked his head as he looked over the York family Halloween decorations. The little trail of ghost lights up along the gutter was all right, but they didn't really work with the dark green color of the house. Too yellow.

The Styrofoam grave markers and broken skeleton in the front yard were much better. Dark gray and spooky. Seemed to fit in, the way the lawn was overgrown.

The witch in the rocking chair up on the front porch? That was the best part. Looked just like a straw-stuffed doll, but Ans and Bishop had tucked a walkie-talkie inside it, so Bishop's mom could give trick-or-treaters a scare after his dad gave them their candy.

Bishop's mom had this awesome witch cackle. Scary as hell.

Ans had just started to wonder what he'd change if he sketched this house when he heard the roar of the Frankencharger's engine, coming around the corner.

Waste of gas, revving the engine like that, but Bish never cared. He ripped into the double-wide driveway like that cop was after him.

But he was smiling when he jumped out of the car, and Ans couldn't help smiling right back at him. Bishop's smile was infectious.

Truth was — and Ans would never admit it — he was jealous of Bishop's looks. The guy was tall and blond, with a chin that could break rocks, and those blue eyes that seemed to make all the girls sigh when he walked down the halls at school.

Far as Ans knew, Bishop never even worked out, but he stayed fit and trim. It just wasn't fair.

Ans was damn near a foot shorter than Bishop. His own black hair never sat straight, and he had to hide his weak chin under a goatee. Plus, Ans would have sworn that eating a three-ounce candy bar could pack ten pounds on his frame.

It just wasn't fair.

The only thing Ans had on Bishop? Physically? Bishop was so pale he could burn in five minutes of direct sun, in the summertime.

Ans' own Portuguese and Ottoman heritage ensured he'd only burn if he forgot sunblock completely.

Wasn't much of an edge, but Ans clung to it.

"Got the blood?" Bishop asked, eager as he always was for Halloween stuff.

Ans patted his backpack.

Bishop threw devil horns, and led the way into the perpetual coffee smell of the York house.

The front yard might have looked like Halloween, but the inside of Bishop's house looked like someone commissioned Norman Rockwell to do a series of cluttered spaces.

The coffee table was covered in gaming and heavy metal mags. The red and blue throw rug on the back of the white leather couch had fallen forward again, puddling on the cushions. Over by the matching loveseat, where Bish's parents watched television in the evenings, a pair of end tables identifiable by their own arrays.

Bish's mom's had a couple of paperback mysteries, plus a collection of gossip and fashion magazines.

Bish's dad's had paperback thrillers, and a spread of sports magazines with an emphasis on football.

Every magazine in the room had been delivered to York Dentistry. Group subscription rate or something.

Down the hall they went, and up the spiral staircase to Bishop's room at the back of the house.

Bish went straight to his closet, but Ans dropped his backpack right inside the door of the room. Puzzled at what he was seeing.

Not that the room was neat. Bed made, books on bookshelves and dresser organized. That just meant that Bishop had been thinking hard about something.

No. It was the walls that were wrong.

Half the pale blue walls were bare. The band posters were still up ... plus the maps of Middle Earth and Westeros...

But Bishop's bikini models. Eight posters, all gone.

"Where are the girls?"

"Yeah," Bishop called out from his closet. "Faye said, and I quote, 'If you don't get rid of the half-naked girls on your walls, you won't get an all-naked Faye on your bed anymore.' Wasn't a tough choice."

Ans frowned. "You guys have been going out for two years, and she said this now?"

Bishop shrugged as he came out of the closet, carrying their thrift store finds. A pair of actual zoot suits, that even almost fit. Dark blue for Bishop, and light gray for Ans. The hats they'd found didn't quite go, but they'd be close enough. Especially once they each had a feather tucked in.

Bishop tossed the suits onto his bed.

"Bish," Ans said, tone expectant.

Bishop sighed. "All right. Faye was never crazy about those posters. But the other night she thought I was looking up at Samantha ... at an inopportune moment."

"Were you?"

"No," Bishop said. "I like looking at *her* while she's doing that. Don't even remember looking away, to be honest. But what was I going to do? Argue?"

"Fair enough," Ans said with a shrug. He dug the tubes of fake blood out of his backpack. "Let's get to work."

The distraction would be a good thing anyway. Ans shuddered to think what *Jewel* would do if she had caught *him* thinking about another girl at a time like that.

"Oh, you would *not*," Faye said, but she was laughing while she said it.

Their phones pinged with word that Bishop was finally done with class, and she fired back a quick *Finally* while Jewel shot off a smiley face.

"Telling you," Jewel said, and clacked her teeth together for emphasis.

Faye and Jewel both dug through the war zone of costume options that remained at Ghosts and Gaffs. It was their fourth stop and their only remaining hope. They'd even managed to fight their way to a corner that was more-or-less just the two of them.

But even where they were, Faye could still hear frustrated parents chasing children who seemed determined to keep every automated decoration going at once.

Dozens of mechanical voices cackled or groaned or droned about blood or danger or just wished the general public a happy Halloween.

Bishop and Anselmo always swore this was the best Halloween store in the area. Certainly it was the biggest. Used to be one of those big, chain bookstores, before some retired magician had turned it into a costume and magic emporium.

Still, Faye didn't like shopping here. Place always smelled like mothballs and candy corn, and the guys behind the counter didn't even try to hide the way they gawked at her.

Or maybe they'd never seen a blond goth before.

"You are *such* a liar," Faye said, flipping past all the obvious choices: nurse, clown, cat, tavern wench — though she bookmarked that one in her mind, Bish would dig it — fairy princess...

"Oh, maybe not *off*," Jewel admitted as she stared hard at the fairy princess costume — the dark reds *would* go well with her dark complexion — "but hard enough that Ans would have learned his lesson. Believe it."

"Ouch," Faye said. Then shook her head as she riffled past a dozen or so superhero costumes, glad that wasn't Bishop's kink.

"I can't believe you tolerated those posters as long as you did," Jewel said, pulling out a slinky black "vampire" dress and holding it up in front of the burnt orange dress she was wearing.

Faye cocked her head, considering. Then shook her head, remembering.

"You did the vampire thing last year. I didn't though..." Faye cocked her head to one side. "Might be too low-cut for me, though. I don't want to fall out while I'm dancing. What do you think?"

Jewel made a show of looking over what Faye was wearing while they shopped: a red velvet top with black lace trim and sleeves, a silver ankh on a black velvet choker, a short black leather skirt and fishnets down to her ankle boots.

"I think if you dressed as a vampire, no one would realize you were wearing a costume."

Faye snorted and pulled out a Cleopatra outfit before returning to the topic.

"Never really thought about his posters before, to be honest." No. Faye knew she was too pale for a dress that white, even with the gold trim to help it. She offered it to Jewel, but Jewel put it right back on the shelf.

"His parents don't like us hanging out in his room," Faye continued as she tried other costumes, "so usually if we're in there, they're gone and Bishop's walls are the last thing on my mind."

"Don't suppose you're finding anything even *close* to a flight attendant's uni," Jewel said, shaking her head at a "sexy dogcatcher" costume.

"Like we'll be that lucky," Faye said.

"Last time I order costumes online," Jewel said, pushing away one rack and digging into another.

That was the shame of it all. Faye and Jewel had planned the perfect costumes weeks ago. They were going to go as Ann and Jana, the deadly flight attendants from *Hell Flight*. It was a pretty obscure horror movie. Nobody else would have thought of it, so they'd be the only ones decked out that way.

Plus, they'd watched it with the boys, so Bish and Ans would definitely have appreciated the costumes.

Even better, according to the site, the costumes they'd found would have been stretchy enough for dancing, and with the jackets, warm enough for wherever the boys were taking them for the Devil's Night stories.

Perfect.

But the company they'd ordered from had lost the order. Never shipped, and too late now to get here in time. They'd refunded the money, but they were still stuck without costumes.

The thing that really sucked about this was that Faye and Jewel could have worn connected costumes again. Just the two of them, like they did when they were little and trick-or-treating.

Faye and Jewel had grown up across the street from each other, and ever since they were tiny they'd been closer than either were with their *actual* sisters.

That they had fallen in love with boys who not only got along, but were best friends was just too perfect.

Their third Halloween, for the four of them. The last two had been about couple costumes, but this year the boys had found those zoot suits.

That meant, to match, Faye and Jewel would have worn old-style dresses. Frilly things, that Faye would have loved and Jewel would have hated, but gone along with to complete the foursome's look.

Faye wouldn't do that to her though. So she'd put her foot down. But the boys had already bought their zoot suits, and she couldn't exactly ask them to find something else.

So, this year, the boys could play their Zoot Suit Riot victims, and Faye and Jewel would find their own look.

Faye paused, finding a costume that would drive Bishop to distraction.

Elf sorceress queen. Gossamer and green, with enough satin underneath for decency. Not *exactly* the look of the elf queen in the online game they all four played together, but close enough that Bishop might have to pick his jaw up off the floor.

It would be cold, though...

"Jewel," Faye said slowly, holding up the costume. "Have you gotten Ans to tell you where the Devil's Night storytelling will be?"

"No," Jewel said though a sigh. "He wants it to be a surprise. And you would *scald* in that."

Faye held it against herself, considered the look in the mirror as Jewel dug through more options. The fabric did bring out the green in her mainly blue eyes. Her Renaissance Faire boots would go great with this outfit. Laced all the way up to the knee, and were soft as calfskin. She could wear her ankh on a silver chain...

"Got it!" Jewel said, so much triumph in her voice that Faye turned to see what she'd found.

Jewel held up a Red Riding Hood costume in one hand, and a "Sexy" Big Bad Wolf costume in the other. (All right, it was technically a "sexy werewolf" costume, but whatever.)

"Like second grade!" Faye said, dropping the elf costume. She reached for the wolf outfit, but Jewel smiled wider and drew it back out of reach.

"Uh uh," she said. "You got to be the wolf last time."

2

OCTOBER 30TH, 7:33 PM.

The dance committee at Long Pine High didn't have much money to work with. At least, to judge by the way the gym was decorated for the dance.

Orange and black streamers. Orange and black balloons. Black crepe paper covering the tables for the snacks and punch. Hand-painted sign letting everyone know the theme: Undead and Loving It.

They'd taken white bedsheets and covered football tackle dummies, trying to make them look like dancing ghosts. Bishop was betting they'd used bent hangars to add the arms and bent knees.

But they'd sprung for dry ice, so there was a gentle layer of fog near the exits, which Bishop had to admit looked pretty cool.

Still smelled like basketball practice had run late. Or maybe ended just before everyone showed up.

At least, though, they had a live band. Surf music with an eerie edge, but kind of cool. And the guitar work was decent, even if *playing* surf music bored Bishop to tears.

Some students were already dancing to the beat, while others were checking out the snacks, the punch, or holding up the walls, like Bishop and Ans.

Though in their case, Bishop and Ans were on their second cups of that fake cherry fruit punch.

The girls weren't here yet.

"Any sign?" Bishop asked, eyes checking the corners in case they'd snuck in, planning a surprise, while Ans watched the entrance.

"Nope," Ans said, adjusting his hat again. Didn't quite fit. And the way they both had their hair slicked back — Bishop's in a high pony-tail he tucked up under his hat — Ans could have ditched the hat.

But then they wouldn't have matched in their fake blood-spattered glory. Blood on their suits trailing from stab wounds, blood on their faces where they'd been slashed by razors.

Bishop took the pocket watch out of his vest pocket and started twirling the fob at the end of the chain. Tried to get his shoulders into just the right position. Faye hadn't seen the costume yet, and he wanted to look perfect when she did.

"Bingo," Ans said, coming up away from the wall.

Bishop turned and smiled while the two of them walked over to meet their dates.

Faye's Little Red Riding Hood dress didn't reach her knees, and showed enough cleavage that no wolf was likely to even notice whether or not she was carrying a basket to her grandmother's house.

"Wow," Ans said, and Bishop could see why. Jewel wore the hell out of that skintight wolf outfit — strategic fur over Spandex — even if her face was hidden under the mask.

"Better watch those claws," Bishop joked, nudging Ans in the ribs. Jewel must have spirit-gummed fur to the back of her hands, and big yellow claws over her nails.

"Give us a spin," Faye said, smiling as Bishop and Ans approached in the strut they'd studied on 'net videos. Shoulders back and hips forward, both twirling their watch fobs.

"Yeah," Jewel added, her voice a little muted by her mask. "Spin."

Bishop spun on his heels. Ans on his toes. Both girls made appreciative noises.

Bishop and Ans each held out a hand at the same time, and whirled their girls out onto the dance floor.

Bishop wasn't any great shakes at dancing. He'd never really learned how. But he had a decent sense of rhythm, thanks to years of guitar, and he wasn't afraid to look like an idiot.

That was something he'd learned, dating Faye. She kind of liked it when he was willing to look like an idiot for her. Rewarded him for it with smiles and kisses. So he'd lost all fear of looking stupid, when she was around.

If Faye hadn't been here, if Bishop had been single, he might have gone the whole night without asking a girl to dance. Too self-conscious. But with Faye by his side, the rest of the world could go hang.

So they twirled and laughed together, through two or three songs — after a while, all the surf songs started to sound alike to Bishop — before she called the halt for some punch.

Ans and Jewel had already staked out a spot on the benches — the bottom three rows of the grandstands were out for students to use — so Faye grabbed punch and Bishop grabbed cookies, and they moved over to join their friends.

Or at least, that was the plan. Right up until John Sorenson got involved.

Sorenson was one of Bishop's least favorite people. He was taller and stronger — blonder, even, with his platinum buzz cut — but that wasn't why. The guy played center for the basketball team, and he lived in the gym. Of course he was taller and stronger.

No, Bishop's problem with Sorenson was Sorenson's problem with him: Faye.

Sorenson and Faye had gone out a few times during freshman year, and Sorenson had never gotten over her. Or at least, he seemed to think that anytime he was single, she would be waiting to come back to him. Whether or not Bishop was in the picture.

So Bishop had his hands full of cookies when he saw Sorenson — dressed as Rambo, to show off his build — grab a cup of punch out of Faye's hands, as though she'd been bringing it to him.

They were on the other side of the table from Bishop, and a

bunch of other kids milled about in the way. Most of them not noticing what was happening yet.

Bishop's feet started moving.

Faye said something — something sharp, no doubt — but Bishop couldn't tell what over the music and conversation. And Sorenson didn't look the least bit put off by her words. He was smiling and saying something.

Bishop started stuffing napkins full of cookies into his pockets as he rounded the long table and closed the distance between them.

Not running. That could lead to—

Sorenson grabbed Faye's wrist, turning like he'd lead her onto the dance floor.

Faye threw her punch in his face and tried to pull her arm away.

Sorenson drew back an arm as though he'd slap her.

Jewel somehow got there first and grabbed that arm.

Bishop, finally there, got between Faye and Sorenson. The other kids around them started chanting, "Fight, fight, fight."

Everything got loud and confused then.

Faye yelling things like, "Let go of my arm," followed by a series of creative insults about Sorenson's parentage and the effects of anabolic steroids.

Jewel was yelling threats of bodily harm if Sorenson didn't let go of Faye.

Bishop was yelling something similar, he was pretty sure. And he definitely had his fists up and ready to go.

Ans showed up too, standing right beside Bishop and ready to keep Sorenson's friends out of the fight or die trying.

And those friends were coming up now. A half-dozen of them, all yelling challenges of their own at Bishop. Their fists by their sides, and their chests puffed out.

Faye got her wrist back.

Bishop shoved Sorenson, but it was like shoving a wall.

Then the fist came.

The fist was Sorenson's. At least, Bishop was pretty sure it had been Sorenson who hit him. That detail was a little fuzzy later.

But that fist caught Bishop square on the jaw.

Felt like a jack had given out, and the whole weight of the Frankencharger had fallen on Bishop's jaw. Pain just exploded outward from that spot.

The hardwood floor of the gym was like a second series of punches when Bishop hit it, first with hips, then his ribs, and then with his head.

THE NEXT FEW MINUTES WERE A BLUR FOR BISHOP. COACHES AND administrators breaking up the "fight." Lots of yelling all around, Faye the loudest.

Bishop was pretty sure he would have been suspended, if Faye and Jewel hadn't been yelling about sexual harassment and threatening legal action. Faye definitely yelled something about a restraining order.

The rest of what she was saying, Bishop didn't quite catch. Faye's parents were both attorneys, and Faye spoke fluent legalese.

Sorenson had his buddies there, backing up his "version" of events — painting Sorenson as the victim, of course — but other girls in the area were right there beside Faye and Jewel. Holding up phones like they'd videoed the whole thing.

Probably did.

And all the while, Bishop had crushed cookies in his pockets and a throbbing pain in his jaw. And he hadn't even gotten to throw a punch.

That stupid shove. What a waste *that* was.

Sorenson got kicked out of the dance, but faced no further punishment. His cronies didn't even get that much.

Disappointing, but not a shock. Not with basketball season coming up.

Bishop got kicked out of the dance too, which seemed most unfair to him. His pathetic attempt at a push should hardly have been counted fighting. Especially compared to that punch.

Worst part? Some comments from one of the gym coaches — Ms. Feeney — about how Faye was showing "too much skin in that outfit," and that Faye would be "lucky" if the worst unwanted grab she got that night was on the *wrist*.

Faye got as far as calling Ms. Feeney a dried up old hag before Principal Null kicked her out of the dance too, along with Jewel and Ans for good measure.

Unlike Sorenson, Bishop, Faye, Ans and Jewel left to scattered applause from the crowd.

Well, the applause were likely for Faye. None of the kids liked Ms. Feeney. Either way, the applause did not improve the principal's mood. He followed Bishop and the others out "to make sure they left school grounds."

Bishop half-suspected Principal Null was making sure that the little confrontation was over. Sorenson was the type to be waiting out here, somewhere. And though he was big, he was only one person, while Bishop's crew was four.

Might have been why the principal didn't kick out Sorenson's friends, now that Bishop thought about it. Would have encouraged Sorenson to come after Bishop with numbers.

Though that would have been giving the principal credit for foresight, which Bishop was loathe to do.

There was at least one good side to Sorenson not getting detention or suspension — if the principal had given Bishop a harsher punishment, he would have had cause to go straight to the school board. With all that video evidence, and likely Faye's parents helping, pro bono.

Still. It wasn't even eight o'clock yet, and, for them, the dance was already over. The four of them walked out into the cool evening air. All the safety lights were on, bathing the parking lot in orange sodium rays that made all four costumes a little more surreal.

The air was still, but Bishop could make out the music of the surf band, though muffled by the concrete walls of the gym. Mainly Bishop could pick out the bass and the lead guitar. The occasional crash cymbal.

Bishop's jaw hurt, his pockets were still full of crushed cookies, and poor Faye and Jewel had barely gotten to dance.

First part of the night's plans, shot straight to hell.

Or was it?

"You know," Bishop said slowly, twining his fingers in with Faye's, "we could have our own dance. Crank up the Frankencharger's stereo, and—"

"What?" Jewel said, and even though Bishop couldn't see her face through that mask, he was sure she had one eyebrow arched. "Mosh?"

"No," Bishop said with a chuckle, but Faye finished for him.

"Bishop doesn't advertise it," she said fondly, "but since we started dating he's been putting together playlists for more romantic scenarios."

"Bish!" Ans mocked. "Your *rep!* The other headbangers won't invite you to their picnics."

"Shut up," Bishop said. "Do you guys want to dance or not? The office park on Middlefield should be empty by now, and the lot's not visible from the street."

Jewel turned to Faye, though her mask looked more goofily threatening than inquisitive.

"No," Faye said through a sigh. She shook her head. "No. Let's get to the horror stories. And at least one of them better include a jock asshole getting ripped apart by something foul."

"I think we can accommodate that," Bishop said, swinging Faye's hand, and turned the group down the right aisle of cars toward the Frankencharger.

"Does this mean we finally get to find out where we're doing this?" Jewel asked.

They all stopped and looked at Ans.

Ans enjoyed the attention. Started with a little half-smile and stroked his goatee.

"Come on!" Bishop said, and the same time Faye added, "Tell us, already!" In the same moment, Jewel chimed in with, "Spill it, buster."

Ans' little smile broke out into a grin. He wiggled his eyebrows. "I found a way inside Colver High."

———

COLVER HIGH.

Bishop figured that pretty much every town had its haunted places. Not just the obvious ones, like cemeteries, but the forgotten places. The abandoned places. Plus the ones with real stories of their own that got dwarfed by the local legends.

Here in Long Pine City, there were a few of them.

Probably the third most haunted, on the list Bishop and Ans kept, was the burnt out church over on Adams. Electrical fire, maybe ... eight years ago? That sounded right to Bishop. He was about ten when his parents were talking about it. According to news reports, the place was empty but for a janitor when it happened, and the janitor got out fine.

Bishop's dad always said it was an insurance fire. That the congregation there had dwindled, and the street was zoned wrong and too busy to unload the land at a decent price.

Whatever.

Every fall, somebody got a keg and there was a party in that church. But the party never lasted that long. Too visible a location, and the cops always came calling before things really got going.

Still, it counted as haunted.

Story the kids all told was that there was a little boy trapped in the place when it went up. Some said the minister's son, others that it was an orphan. Either way, he was supposed to have snuck in to practice the organ. After the fire, the church had paid the janitor to cover it up.

Story said that if you snuck in on a moonless night, you might still hear the kid playing Beethoven.

If you did, you had to clear out. Because the moment he finished his song, he'd come for you.

Bishop and Ans had held their Devil's Night storytelling there in eighth grade, but Suzi Jenkins and Darla Hopkins, the first girls invited to join them, had declared it cold and creepy and a stupid idea.

They hadn't heard any spooky classical music, but they hadn't been there all that long either.

The second most haunted place in Long Pine City was a field, down near the shopping center. The one anchored by that big ugly box store.

The real story that Bishop had been able to find said that three homeless guys got knifed there one night, back in the 70s. Drug deal gone wrong, according to the police report.

Either way, it was a bloody business, and the local kids took over the legend from there.

Story now went that there'd been four homeless guys there that night. And that, together, they'd been digging themselves a little latrine and found a small box of Wells Fargo gold, from the stage-coach days.

Three of them were eager to share their good fortune, but one got a little too greedy...

Story is, the gold got lost in the struggle, and the killer still lives down there. Eats what gets thrown away at the nearby fast food places. Sleeps down around the creeks by day. And spends his nights hunting for his gold, and killing anyone who gets in his way.

Another version, the one Bishop preferred, said that the fourth guy got away from the fight, but was bleeding badly. Made it as far as the salt flats across the freeway, and died out there. His body was never found, of course. Eaten by coyotes, maybe.

Either way, his spirit still returns to that one field every night, hunting for its lost gold.

Bishop always liked the touch about the gold. Especially since the old stagecoach route did go through Long Pine City on its way to San Francisco. Gave the story a real *could-it-be?* vibe.

Bishop and Ans had held their Devil's Night storytelling out there in seventh grade. Field was creepy enough, to be sure, but they never saw or heard anybody, living or dead.

Well, *Ans* swore he saw someone moving by an old, abandoned refrigerator, but Bishop didn't believe it. Figured Ans got spooked by the high grass or something.

Still, the prize for most haunted site in Long Pine City had to go to Colver High. That one might have been more than just a story told by the local kids.

Part of the reason Bishop thought so was that there were so many stories about Colver. The other supposedly haunted sites in town, they all had pretty much one story each. Maybe little variations and embellishments, but one primary storyline.

Colver, though.

Some kids said they had to close it when a psychiatric patient escaped from nearby Saint Josephine's Hospital and ran amok with a fire axe.

Others, maybe influenced by the church incident, said that the place caught fire during a pep rally, and half the school burned alive.

That there was no sign of fire damage from the outside didn't deter these stories in the least.

Some said the place had been haunted from the time it was built. That it was built on the site of a mass grave, used by the railroad to dump Chinese workers who'd worked themselves to death.

Some said the site had been cursed by witches.

Others that when the Catholic missionaries had come through the area, they'd found a native tribe that they considered unsaveable. Cannibalism, incest and worse. So they'd slaughtered the entire tribe, and the site just happened to get later used for Colver High.

On and on the stories went. All of them agreeing that Colver High was haunted by something evil and mightily pissed off.

Bishop and Ans, naturally, had tried to find out all the could.

There hadn't been much they could find, and that just made the site even more curious. They'd gone through the old microfiche files at the Gazette, the county recorder's office, everything they could think of.

What they *had* been able to learn?

There'd once been two high schools in Long Pine City. Long Pine High, and Colver.

Colver had closed down in the 50s. No reason given.

Just how weird was that? No reason given?

Bishop's parents said that it was a problem in the natural gas pipes, but that the flaw had been discovered before anything terrible had happened.

According to them, the flaw was too basic to be fixed cheaply. The city would have had to redo the entire foundation. Or maybe just demolish the school, and start from scratch.

The city had been arguing for decades about what to do with Colver. Different groups wanted to turn it into a community center, or a hospital, or something more than an eyesore, at least.

According to news reports the city didn't want to sell the land to developers, because of a zoning issue about housing density, and the main interest they could get was from people wanting to build condos.

Bishop's mother — whose family had lived here in Long Pine City since the early 1900s — said that the real problem wasn't zoning. It was the land-use permit.

That had gotten Bishop and Ans on their bikes and down to the county recorder's office.

And sure enough, Mom had a point.

Turned out that the land was actually owned by the Rutherford family, some of the oldest money in the Bay Area. Real gold rush tycoons.

Edmund Rutherford had signed an exclusive, one-hundred-year lease with the city back around the end of World War I, at a historically low rate. But stipulated that the city could only use the land for a high school, and if they tried to repurpose it, they had to renegotiate or lose the lease.

Big on education, the Rutherfords.

Bishop didn't know what any of that meant about why the school closed, except that as far as he was concerned, the Rutherford ownership was a point he made sure to work into the legends, whenever he told them.

Bishop and Ans had managed to slip through the cyclone fence to tell Devil's Night stories on the lawn, back among the trees, when they were in sixth grade.

But they'd never managed to get inside.

JOHN SORENSON CROUCHED BESIDE HIS CAMARO IN THE COOL EVENING air.

Not because he was afraid of that limp-prick York or his friend Magellan. No, he didn't hide from any guy, much less a couple of dweebs like those two.

Heck, just thinking about them made Sorenson's knuckles tingle, and a smile spread across his face.

Getting tossed from the dance had been worth it, for getting to deck that prick, York. Only way it would have been better would have been if he'd gotten to lay into Magellan too.

Bishop and Anselmo. Were there any stupider names in the world? Sorenson still couldn't fathom how those losers had managed to catch and hold the interest of a couple of major hotties like Faye and Jewel.

Sure, York had that bitch hair, like he thought he was some great rocker or something. But what else did he have to offer, anyway? All right, he got good grades, but so what?

Sorenson already had *three scholarship offers* for next year. *Full rides.* And the senior season hadn't even started yet. What did *York* have, besides that stupid car?

Sorenson was *going* places. York, he was going *nowhere.* Loser was even taking Auto Shop. Probably just an excuse to get stoned on campus.

What the hell did Faye see in him?

The four of them were only two cars away, here in the student parking lot, talking about dancing. Close enough that Sorenson imagined he could smell that flowery body wash Faye used.

Used to use. Maybe still did.

Truth was, Sorenson hadn't been close enough to know for sure. Not for a couple of years now. Not since she'd started seeing York.

Sorenson had figured those two wouldn't last a month. Two years later, they were still dating?

Didn't add up.

Maybe he was blackmailing her or something.

Faye. She looked mouth-watering in that Little Red Riding Hood getup.

If Long Pine High had a queen, it was her. Even when she wore her ghostly, goth makeup, she was still the most beautiful girl in school by a long shot. Smart too. And funny. Who knew a hot girl could be funny?

And that *body*...

Truth was, *Faye* was the reason Sorenson was hiding.

Made one mistake already tonight. Didn't need a second.

He never should have grabbed her wrist. What the hell had he been thinking? Faye wasn't the kind of girl who went for that sort of assertive treatment. Not like Lisa O'Leary. That girl couldn't get enough of the rough stuff.

Sorenson could have dragged Lisa O'Leary onto the dance floor by her *hair* and she would still have loved it.

No excuse though.

Neither was the Jameson's Sorenson had shared with Cruiser and the boys in the lot before the dance.

Oh, sure, the Jameson's was probably the *reason* Sorenson had done it — he felt pretty sure of that. He'd been spending so much time with Lisa lately that he got a little of the old Irish in his system and just didn't think before he tried to drag Faye onto the dance floor to see if his sweet moves could win her back.

But that was no *excuse*.

Probably a good thing Jewel had got there before he slapped Faye.

A grab on the wrist, Sorenson could probably talk his way past that. If he could get her away from Bishop for a few.

Sorenson knew how to turn on the old charm.

But a slap? On a girl like Faye?

That would have been it for him, boy.

Wait.

Did Sorenson hear that right?

Those four were going to Colver? Seriously?

Now?

What kind of useless losers were York and Magellan anyway? They get kicked out the dance early, and instead of taking their hotties out to a motel — or at least Skyline or one of the other make-out spots — they want to go look at the abandoned high school?

And what did Magellan mean by Devil's Night? What the hell was that? He and York some kind of Satanists?

Sorenson sneaked a glance over the hood of his Camaro.

Well, whatever "Devil's Night" was, all four of them were piling into that broken down Charger of York's. Faye included.

She was even smiling. Like running out to *Colver* with York was some kind of treat.

Had they found a way inside?

Man, *that alone* would be worth following them. Sorenson and his pals must have tried a dozen times to break into that old dump. But the windows were all double-paned, with chicken wire in between. And they'd been nailed shut from the inside or something. No give at all.

And the padlocks on the doors were the real deal. Even ten whacks with a hammer couldn't get Sorenson past one of those things. And any more would have drawn the cops.

Could York and Magellan have found a way in?

Probably not. Probably just wanted to do it on the grass, where the trees would hide them from the road. That sounded classy enough for York, since it seemed he was too cheap or too broke to spring for a night at the Sleep Tite.

Of course, the idea of a doofus like York getting to do *anything* with Faye was something Sorenson didn't want to think about.

But what if they *had* found a way inside?

What if York and Magellan had set up housekeeping in there or something? Their own private little make-out joint. Maybe with their own bottles of booze tucked away. Thrift store mattresses. Camp lanterns...

Yeah. Sorenson could just see how he'd do it up right, if he were the one setting up the joint.

And the more he thought about it, while York's Charger pulled out of the parking lot — at boring, old-man speeds that were probably fast as the POS could go — the more likely it seemed.

York and Magellan, they were the kind who'd throw serious effort at a problem like how to get inside Colver. Wasn't like they had anything better to do with their time.

Probably really did turn it into their little clubhouse, or whatever.

Probably felt comfortable as hell in there.

Yeah. Sorenson could see it now.

Maybe York had found the one window with some give. Faye'd get her Red Riding Hood costume all dirty going in, but he wouldn't care. Not so long as he got some—

Hey. Wasn't Colver supposed to be haunted? Like that burned out church or something?

Yeah, that was right. Sorenson was sure he'd heard a story about that place. Something about missionaries burning cannibal Indians.

Well. Maybe tonight was looking up after all.

Yes. Maybe tonight those Indians would rise from the grave for some payback against York. And maybe, if Sorenson played it right, he could scare Faye right into his own arms...

Sorenson knew just what he needed.

He pulled out his phone and started firing off texts.

3

———

Bishop didn't park next to Colver. This time of year, the cops would be *expecting* kids to try to break into someplace as cool as an abandoned high school.

So he couldn't park anyplace that might draw attention.

Instead, he parked down the street and just around the corner from the weak spot in the cyclone fence that he and Ans had found a few years back. Probably the same one all the kids used, when they were of a mind to try something like this.

That spot had the advantage of being near the grove of trees on the campus. Cut down on visibility, when it came to sneaking in.

Hell, cops probably used the same weak spot when they came in to check for kids doing it or toking up among the trees.

He killed the engine — and the sounds of Volbeat's "Seal the Deal" — and turned a big smile on Faye, who gave him a big smile right back.

She looked a little flush around the cheeks. Her pulse was probably racing, same as his was. She loved adventure as much as he did. And Bishop could feel his skin in that cool way he felt it whenever he was excited. As though suddenly the air all around his body became more tangible. His stomach had that good kind of flutter, too.

The chance to go where none of the other kids had been. The risk of getting caught.

Just the thrill of sneaking into this place would be awesome. Even not counting the stories.

Hell, Bishop was so jazzed already he could barely feel the ache in his jaw. Might have forgotten the dance entirely, if not for the fake cherry taste of punch on his tongue.

He pulled Faye's hand up and kissed her knuckles, getting a warm look and a small sound of pleasure for his efforts.

"Hey, you two," Jewel said from the backseat. She was easier to understand now that she'd ditched the wolf mask. "Stories first. Make out later."

"Right," Bishop said, while Faye mouthed, "Later."

He opened the door and stepped out into the night air. Cool, but not too cold. Clear sky full of stars up above, and a three-quarters moon. Probably be plenty of light, even once they got away from the streetlights.

Might not even need flashlights until they got inside.

The street around them was pretty quiet. Must not have been a lot of kids on this block. Half the porch lights were off, and only maybe a third of the houses done up for Halloween.

Was a party going down the block, though. Bishop could hear some kind of bass beat, and there was less available parking down that way. Plus one house was lit up *bright*.

Bishop wondered who was partying there while Ans pushed the seat forward and followed him out onto the asphalt. Bishop locked his door — Faye would handle hers, of course — and stepped around to pop the trunk.

"Just the flashlights," Ans said while the trunk creaked open. "We'll want them in case we need them before we get inside."

"We won't need the blankets?" Bishop asked, his hands already on the padded moving blankets he kept clean in case of an outdoor opportunity.

Faye loved spontaneity. She still talked about the time he surprised her with a picnic up on Skyline, even though he'd made sure to keep the surprises coming since then.

Maybe she was angling for another picnic? He'd have to keep that in mind.

"Nope. No blankets needed," Ans said, and even held up a forestalling hand when Bishop grabbed the bottle of Moreno Tequila he kept in the wheel well.

"Seriously," Ans said with a smile. "I've covered everything."

Bishop pulled out four small L.E.D. flashlights and distributed them before closing the trunk with as soft a thunk as he could manage.

He turned to Ans. "Lay on, MacDuff."

"Lay on?" Jewel interrupted. "I mean, I know that's the right quote from *Macbeth*, but—"

"We used to say 'lead on, MacDuff,' when we were kids," Ans said, taking Jewel's arm and leading down the street, while glancing at a piece of paper like he was looking at directions.

Idea was, anyone who glanced over would think they were looking for an address.

"Then my mom heard us," Bishop chimed in, "and corrected us. Eighth grade, wasn't it?"

"Yep," Ans confirmed.

"But 'lay on' doesn't make sense in this context," Faye said, though she was still smiling as she squeezed Bishop's arm. "Unless you're telling him to attack you."

"We know," Bishop said with a shrug.

"We just think it's funny," Ans said.

Jewel shook her head, one eyebrow high, but Faye actually chuckled softly.

"You are *so* weird," Faye whispered, but she sounded like she approved.

Just past halfway down the block, Ans raised his arm, pointed, and gestured to the right. As though the place they were looking for was down the street and just around the corner from the old high school.

That was the signal to cut across the street.

They hustled across, laughing despite themselves.

Ans grabbed the loose spot in the cyclone fence, where it lost connection to its pole. Wriggled through, then held it wider while Jewel and Faye slipped through. Bishop came last, catching up as the others padded quickly across the thick grass toward the grove of long pines and out of sight.

As soon as Bishop was inside the tree line, Ans whispered, "Wait. Let our eyes adjust."

Funny. Bishop hadn't thought there was all that much light out on the street, but here under the cover of the trees, it looked almost pitch black.

Yeah, he could have pulled out his flashlight, but they were still too near the street. Someone might—

Headlights.

"Car!" Bishop whispered, and ducked behind the nearest tree.

He tripped over a root. Went down on a bed of pine needles. Reminded him he still had cookies in his pockets, and gave him an up-close-and-personal scent of pine.

Didn't move though. Tried not to breathe.

Worst part? He could *hear* Ans trying not to laugh. His breaths all jagged and loud through his nose.

Didn't know where Faye was, though. Not until he felt her hand squeeze his shoulder.

"Car's gone," she whispered. She was crouched beside him, and Bishop's adjusting pupils showed that she was handing him his hat.

Couldn't see her expression though. Not yet.

Bishop took the hat and used it to dust himself off as he stood. He'd fallen forward, so his front was covered with pine needles.

Hands brushed his back anyway, starting with his shoulders and working their way down, paying special attention to his butt and thighs.

"I don't think I got any needles back there," he said softly.

"Best to be sure," Faye said, giving his butt a squeeze for good measure.

Jewel cleared her throat.

Faye made a show of raising her empty hands.

Bishop realized he could now see well enough to make out the shapes of all his friends, plus a decent look at the trees and ground around him.

The world was shades of gray, but he could see it. Well enough, even, that he spotted the root he tripped over.

Not a lot of bushes or undergrowth out here though. Just the long pines. Bishop wasn't sure whether that was normal or strange.

"This way," Ans said, and led them between trees through the grove, followed by Jewel, then Faye, then Bishop. All four holding hands, like a chain.

None of them were exactly outdoorsy. They made a pretty good racket, snapping twigs and crunching dried pine needles.

In fact, they were maybe a third of the way across when a voice stage whispered, "Hey. You guys wanna toke?"

The moment he heard the voice, Bishop saw the cherry at the end of the joint, ahead and to the right. And he could smell the herb.

Not that he was tempted. He and Ans had tried pot a couple of times, but it never really did much for either of them.

Bishop couldn't get a good look at the guy offering. He stood maybe fifteen feet off to one side. Little shorter than Bishop, and heavier through the gut.

But the guy could have been their age, or even a decade older, there in the dim moonlight beneath the grove of long pines.

Bishop thought he saw movement, too. Like the guy wasn't out here alone.

"No thanks," Ans answered. "We've got, uh, *other* plans tonight."

"You sure? I got plenty."

"We're sure," Jewel answered, in tones that left no doubt about her meaning.

The guy gave a sleazy kind of laugh. "There's a good spot about two hundred feet farther along. Little patch of grass still covered from the street by the trees. Nobody'll bother you there."

"We know the spot," Jewel said. "*Just* where we were heading. Maybe we'll see you later."

"Be here most of the night," the guy added, and Bishop was pretty sure he leered at Jewel and Faye.

But then Ans was moving, and the four of them continued along, still managing to see just well enough in the moonlight that filtered through the trees that they didn't need their flashlights.

Good. Bishop didn't want to be easy to follow. Just in case the stoners weren't as cool as they tried to come across.

They passed that little clearing, where the patch of grass was bent down as though others had used it already tonight.

They kept moving.

Finally, they made it out of the trees, and Bishop got his first good look at Colver High in more than two years.

After the darkness of the grove of long pines, the bright moonlight made Bishop's eyes ache.

That moon seemed to light up the old Colver High School building like daylight.

Colver High.

Place was built like a giant box made of red brick. Like someone had sketched out a rectangle on the ground, then stretched it three stories straight up. Hardly any decoration to it. Maybe little crenellations at the corners. But if it had ever been painted, the paint had worn away through decades of weather, leaving only the dirty bricks underneath.

Small windows on the first floor, and all of them looked to be above head height. But on the upper two floors, tall, wide windows.

As though the top two floors were the only ones that really deserved light.

Wide, round steps led up to the main doors, in the center of the long side. Looked like the kind of place Bishop could imagine the principal standing to address the entire school.

In fact, those stairs were wide enough that they could have served as the stage for commencement exercises. Bishop could just picture rows of folding chairs set up on the huge swath of lawn before those stairs, filled with students in caps and gowns, and proud parents in old timey getups.

The doors at the top of those stairs weren't the only entrance, either. Bishop remembered, from the scouting mission he and Ans had come on, back when they first tried to figure out if they could get inside.

On the short sides of the box shape, simpler staircases led to less impressive double-doors.

Three total entrances, all with stairs.

Bishop's dad would have called this place an OSHA nightmare. His mom would have called it a firetrap.

Bishop thought it almost looked like a warehouse.

Almost.

After all, most warehouses didn't have a bell tower.

Dead center of the roof. Built out of narrowing, ridged bubbles of grayish concrete, right up to the bell itself.

Bishop wondered at that. In the brightness of the moonlight — fading fast, now that his eyes were adjusting again — he could see that the bell was still there.

Shouldn't they have taken that thing down?

Then again, the whole place probably *should* have been demolished. A brick building in California? Earthquake capital of the United States? No wonder there were problems with the foundation.

It was like *asking* for trouble.

Even weirder, the place was supposed to have been built after 1906, so there was no excuse. The rest of the Bay Area learned not to build with brick after the quake of '06.

So what was the deal here?

A question for later, maybe.

"We're at the wrong end," Ans said, only just loud enough for the others to hear him. "We want the south side doors."

They'd come out of the grove about midway between the main entrance and the north end of the building.

Ans took Jewel's hand and started to lead around toward the south side, but Bishop cleared his throat. Nodded his head back toward the woods.

One advantage to having been friends with Ans for so many years. They didn't always need to explain what they were thinking. A single nod was all Bishop needed, to remind Ans, "Hey, one of those stoners might have followed us. We shouldn't head straight for our entrance."

Ans started leading around the north side of the building. Faye and Bishop right behind him. Bishop keeping watch over his shoulder, to make sure no one followed out of the woods.

Ans and Jewel were a few steps ahead of Bishop and Faye now, whispering to each other about something.

"God," Faye said, quietly enough that Bishop only barely heard her. "The place just smells decrepit."

Bishop smelled grass and pine and night air. Gave her a curious look, but Faye's eyes were still on the building.

"What do you mean?" he whispered.

"Oh," Faye said a little louder, reddening at the cheeks. "Nothing."

"Come on," Bishop said, swinging her hand a little harder. "You're always quick to point out how weird *I* am."

"I am *not* weird." Faye broke out in a smile. "All right. I am. Kind of. Sometimes."

"So, spill it. What do you mean? You can smell that place from here?"

"Not ... exactly," she said. "It's just. How do I say it? I pick things up sometimes. Things other people don't."

"What," Bishop said, trying not to sound suspicious. Only encouraging. "Like you're psychic?"

"*God*," she said, shaking her head. Quieter she added, "I did *not* say that. And don't let Jewel hear *you* say it."

"All right, all right," Bishop said. "What do you mean then?"

She went quiet then, while they rounded the north end of the main building. Around the west side, there was a smaller building. If anything, it was even boxier and more boring than the main building. He was pretty sure it was an old gym.

Like the main building, it was built strictly by economy. One set of double-doors leading in. Hardly any windows, and the ones it had were all way high up.

Those windows were all broken, which was interesting. Sure, there were some busted windows on the main building, but they were harder to spot because of the thick chicken wire tucked between the panes.

Bishop always wondered about that. Were they that worried about people breaking in, back a hundred years ago or whatever?

Or where they more interested in making sure the students didn't escape?

That was an interesting thought, while Bishop glanced over his shoulder again, to make sure he didn't see anyone following them.

Of course, with the trees where they were, it would have been easy enough to hide, at this point. Around the west side of the building, though, it would be harder. Anyone following would become visible in the moonlight as they rounded the end of the building, or they'd risk losing Bishop's group.

"It's like this," Faye said, bringing Bishop's attention back to their conversation, as they walked slowly down the sidewalk that surrounded the main building.

"I've always been ... intuitive. I pick things up about people. Places. Doesn't happen all the time. I can't choose when it happens. And sometimes, I have to meet a person or go to a place more than once before I pick up anything."

"Can you give me an example?"

"I'll give you two," she said, flashing Bishop a bright smile. "First one, Sorenson. Took me three dates to get a flash on what kind of person he really was, when he wasn't turning on the charm."

"You mean an asshole?"

"Yes and no," Faye said with a frown. "He's a sad case, to tell you the truth. But it doesn't matter, because he drags people into darkness."

She shook her head. "Definitely not my idea of boyfriend material."

"Okay," Bishop said, welling up with a little pride that he made the cut. "What's the other example?"

She cocked an eyebrow at him. "Do I really need to say it?"

Bishop frowned, then understanding hit him and he smiled. But he had to try to cover that gap. Wouldn't do to look slow in front of Faye.

"Maybe I want to hear it."

"All right," she said. "Remember the moment you first asked me out? Back at the end Mr. Hooper's World History class?"

Bishop nodded. Of course he remembered. He'd been so nervous his palms wouldn't stop sweating, and he'd needed three deep breaths just to get the nerve to approach her.

"Well the moment you opened your mouth, I got a flash on what kind of guy *you* really are."

"What kind is that?"

"The kind I like best," she said, and swung his hand a little harder.

Bishop had the feeling that was all the answer he was going to get. But that was all right.

It was answer enough.

ANS LOVED THE WAY HIS GUTS WERE DANCING WITH EXCITEMENT AS HE led Jewel around the south corner of the Colver High main building, and to the set of stairs waiting there.

The night was perfect. Not too cold. Brisk. Just enough chill to set his skin on edge, out here where the breeze could tickle a little. Just rustle the trees, and add the smell of autumn.

More than half a moon, but still that basic headsman's-axe shape he loved.

Closer to midnight would have been better. But this was close enough.

Weeks of planning had gone into this night. Starting with this moment. Hours and hours of effort.

And it was all, finally coming together.

He couldn't wait to see their expressions. Hear their excitement. How impressed they'd be. Couldn't wait to reveal his surprises.

Especially to Jewel.

Bishop liked to talk about how much Faye liked surprises? Well, Faye had *nothing* on Jewel. Good surprises got Jewel going better than anything else.

And tonight would be a series of excellent surprises.

"All right," he said, flattening against the dirty bricks as he glanced around the corner.

That was purely for effect. He'd checked the lines of sight two days ago.

From where he stood, against the corner of the building, nobody was likely to see him. This spot was a good hundred yards of lawn from the cyclone fence.

And better than cyclone fence, there was a little row of elms along the street on that side, just outside the fence. Planted by the neighbors a few decades back, they now stood tall enough to help cut down on the eyesore factor of having an abandoned high school across the street.

And on the south side, they were a little thicker and fuller than on the north side.

That was why Ans had chosen the south side.

Sure, in terms of street visibility, the east side would have been best. The grove of long pines and all. But he hadn't been able to count on the idea of the grove being empty on a Friday night.

He'd been right, too. He loved it when his plans worked right.

So he'd picked the south side. Good enough concealment to give them time to get inside without risk of being seen. Even the first surprise of the evening.

Well, second. The first was that they were here at all.

"All right," Ans said again. Softly this time. "Coast is clear. Bish. Check the door."

Bishop slipped past Ans with a respectable effort at stealth. He padded up the concrete steps.

"No good," Bishop said. "They're chained and locked, like last time."

Ans *almost* spoke up. But he knew Bishop pretty well. If Ans waited just a moment longer...

"Gets worse," Bishop said. "The lock looks new. Looks like someone found your way in and—"

"Try this," Ans said, tossing Bishop a key.

Bishop's jaw dropped like it did that during that first beach trip, the summer after sophomore year. The first time he saw Faye in a bikini.

A weird comparison. Weirder still was wondering which of them enjoyed the reaction more.

But Bishop caught the key. Frowned at Ans, but tried it.

"Son of a bitch," Bishop said. But he unlocked the padlock, and unwound the chain with respectable speed while the others joined him on the stairs.

Bishop pulled the door open, smooth and quiet as though someone had oiled it just yesterday.

Which, of course, Ans had done.

The girls went through first, but then Bishop. Ans closed the doors behind them and dropped the chain on the floor just inside the door.

The padlock he tucked into his vest pocket, alongside his pocket watch.

He turned, and watched the other three flick on their flashlights and examine the hallway.

He knew how it must have looked to them.

Scary.

The hallway was wider than expected. And the tiles were dust-covered, but still intact. And they carried every echo. Magnified all of it.

The walls along the inside were concrete, not drywall. Just like the stairwell inside the door, that led to the two upper floors. All that concrete added its own opinion to the echoes of the door closing.

"Hello," Ans called softly, and the word came back sounding distant and just a little sinister. Just enough to raise the hairs on the back of his neck. And maybe do that to the others too.

"How?" Bishop asked.

"What?" Ans said with a smile he knew was smug. "The echoes? It's all—"

"Reflective surfaces," Bishop finished for him. "Don't lecture a musician on sound. How did you get the key for that lock?"

"I bought the lock," Ans said, smiling wider now.

"Ans."

Ans bet his teeth were visible even without a flashlight beam on them. He reached into his pocket and pulled out his lock picks.

Bishop started to chuckle.

"And *why* exactly," Jewel asked, hands on her hips, "do you have *those*?"

"Entirely for tonight, I assure you."

"You bought those things two years ago," Bishop said, "and you never—"

"I bought them after Faye and Jewel brought stories to our first Devil's Night together, to be precise," Ans said. "Because I knew I wanted to surprise them one day by sneaking them in here. Remember how we'd pulled at those locks when we first tried it, Bish?"

Bishop nodded.

"Well, I'd snuck back later and wrote down the make and model of those padlocks." Ans was getting into his story now, letting relish fill his voice as he continued. "Then I went into forums for lock pick enthusiasts."

He turned to Jewel. "People do it as a hobby, you know. Not just criminals."

She lifted an imperious eyebrow. "Do they?"

All the joy rushed out of Ans, fleeing ahead of a sense of cold fear. "Seriously. I can show you sites. My internet history."

"You may not want to see his internet history," Bishop said, like he was missing all of Jewel's warning signs.

"Shut up, Bish," Ans said, not looking away from Jewel. He pleaded with his hands. "Honest. It was all for this. I'll throw them away tonight, if you want."

Faye leaned in and whispered something in Jewel's ear. Jewel nodded absently, then let her eyebrow drop. "Go on. You went into forums."

"Right. Forums," Ans said, but he was sweating now. Nervous. "I found a lock exchange program, where people would trade locks to practice on. I'd picked up a bunch from local thrift stores, and listed them all as available to trade, if someone could send me one of the same make and model used on the south side door."

"Took about six months, but I found one." He shrugged. "Then it was just time and practice. Once I had it though, it was easily to slip down here and pick this one. Then I replaced it with one I knew even better, just in case."

Ans gave Jewel a hopeful smile, but she gave him a stone face back.

Ans was tempted to keep talking. Just hoping he'd happen across the right words. But he knew better. She had to be the one to talk next.

"So you expect me to believe you did *all this*. Learned to pick locks, haunted lock picker forums for months. All for this one surprise?"

Ans nodded, trying not to let the pounding of his heart sound like a doom march in his ears.

"Sounds to me like I've got a pretty darn thoughtful boyfriend," she said with a slow smile. "Do you have any more surprises for me, baby?"

"Right this way."

He led them down the hall, making sure to highlight a few things with his own flashlight.

The red door of the third classroom along. The one with the scratches all over it. Even high up. Like a dog as big as an Irish wolfhound had tried to claw its way in.

"Think it was a werewolf?" Ans asked. "What do you think, Jewel? You're the resident expert."

"I'm big and bad for a wolf," Jewel said, voice teasing. "But I'm not a werewolf."

Still, she took her costume claws and mimed slashing at the door.

"Wonder why they had a dog—" Bishop started, but Faye answered before he finished.

Faye had a funny look as she spoke then. Distant. Like she was seeing something no one else could see.

"Someone wasn't supposed to be in there," Faye said. Hushed, and a little sad. Like she was at a funeral. She shivered. "Don't go in there. Please."

Jewel was frowning at Faye. "Don't you start that, Ms. Sees—"

"I won't," Faye said firmly, frowning right back at Jewel. "But don't *you* go in someplace I say not to."

"I'll go where I—"

"Hey," Ans said softly, stepping between them. "Our tour doesn't go in here anyway. It's this way, all right?"

He looked from one girl to the other, but his focus was on Jewel, while Bishop whispered something into Faye's ear.

Faye nodded.

Jewel nodded, but still gave Faye narrow eyes.

Ans took Jewel's free hand, and started leading her down the hall. Bishop and Faye fell into step behind them.

The next thing he showed them was only a few steps farther down the hall. Old playbills for a school production of *Macbeth*.

He lit his face from below and turned a smile on Bishop. "And damned be him..."

"...who first cries hold! Enough!" Bishop answered.

Faye and Jewel looked at each other, frowning differently now. A shared, puzzled kind of frown, which Ans admittedly preferred to the other kind.

"It's the rest of the line," Bishop said.

"'Lay on, Macduff,'" Ans quoted, "and damned be him who first cries hold! Enough!'"

"Enough with the Shakespeare," Jewel said, but Ans thought he saw Faye pull Bishop's arm a little tighter.

"Onward," Ans said, leading farther down.

He didn't stop them again until he got to the most important room here.

This one had brown wooden doors. Two of them. And though they locked, they hadn't been locked when Ans found them.

He turned to the others with a flourish.

"We're here."

BISHOP COULD HARDLY BELIEVE IT. HE WAS STANDING *INSIDE* COLVER High School. In one of the main hallways, outside an important-looking set of double-doors.

Well, important in that they were the only double-doors so far on the floor. Plus, they were on the east side, and only maybe a quarter of the way down the building.

Bishop figured that was just on the edge of the offices of the administration. At least, if Colver had been laid out anything like Long Pine High.

Ans had really outdone himself this time.

The ancient hardwood floor and the ceilings weren't exactly *clean*, but they weren't nearly as dusty and dirty as Bishop would have expected. Yes, he could smell the age, but he wasn't kicking up dust clouds with every step, much less stepping on the bodies of dead rats or something.

Ans had to have swept the route in. Only explanation. Didn't want to blow the mood by getting the girls' costumes dirty.

And now Ans smiled like a ringmaster. Or maybe a stage magician about to open the box to show that his assistant had disappeared. His hands on the knobs of the double-door. Hesitating for dramatic effect before opening them.

Bishop shook his head. The bit with Jewel and the lock picking had been close for a moment, but even so. Ans was enjoying this way too much. The werewolf thing, and the dried, torn old Macbeth playbills.

Bishop hoped whatever lay on the other side was in better shape than those playbills, though. Even with the sweeping Ans must've done, Bishop was smelling too much dust and decay in this place.

Telling ghost stories here, that seemed natural. But Ans had implied that the evening's ... other activities could take place here too.

Bishop wasn't sure about Jewel, but he knew *Faye* wouldn't be in the mood if the make-out spot was nasty and dusty. Or worse, mildewed.

Faye was allergic to mildew. Not conducive to romance.

No. Bishop had to put his trust in Ans. He'd done almost everything right so far.

Ans pushed open those wooden doors, and stepped back with a flourish, while Bishop, Faye and Jewel all covered the room with the beams of their flashlights.

The room was way better than anything Bishop expected.

First, it was big. Easily thirty feet across, and twenty feet wide. The walls were dirty and yellowed, but they were better than raw brick. Stucco, maybe, with residue in places where there might once have been wallpaper.

The floor in here had been swept even more thoroughly than the hallway. And there was some kind of floral smell to the air. Like Ans had been hitting it with air fresheners or something.

There were old couches, not desks, and they'd been pushed off to one side and covered with drop cloths.

At least, Bishop *assumed* the shapes under the drop cloths were couches. They had the right shape.

There were two low coffee tables — redwood maybe — that had

been pushed together in the center of the room. Arrayed on the coffee tables, a small collection of sliced cheeses and chocolates, in zipped up sandwich bags. Four white pillar candles as well. Currently unlit, but the lighter was sitting beside them.

Also, two bottles of wine, a corkscrew, four plastic wine glasses, and a roll of paper towels.

Surrounding the coffee tables, four sleeping bags, zipped open for sitting comfort, but Bishop imagined the intention for later was to move them off to private corners.

Most of the rest of the room was empty. There was a taller table though — like a rectangular kitchen table — pressed against the wall at one side, under an old corkboard.

Nothing on the corkboard. Not even old pins.

In a corner of the room, a wooden door, with a little sign on it reading "restroom."

"This was the teachers' lounge, I think," Ans said. "When I first found it, I could still smell old cigarette smoke, even over the dust."

"Did you sweep this place?" Jewel asked as her flashlight beam tracked across the wooden floor.

"Didn't want to get you all dusty," Ans said with a smile.

"I have the best boyfriend ever," Jewel said, tilting Ans' face to hers for a kiss, while Bishop and Faye selected their sleeping bag. The one they sat on had a red flannel interior, and felt padded.

Bishop started laying out cheeses and chocolates on paper towels, giving Jewel a moment to thank Ans properly for his efforts, but Faye looked at the wine and said, "Jewel? It's a Red Raven pinot."

The kiss stopped, because Jewel started laughing, in a good way.

"Seriously," Jewel, said, laughter still in her voice as she led Ans over to the table. "Did I build you in a lab or something?"

Ans reached for the lighter to light the candles, but Bishop said, "We better not." Pointed up toward the windows. "Don't want to risk anyone seeing candlelight flickering on the ceiling."

"Really?" Ans asked, picking up his flashlight. "I'm not sure anyone could even see a flashlight beam."

He turned his beam onto the windows before Bishop could stop him—

—and started laughing. He'd tacked up black cloths over the windows.

"How did you even get *up* there?" Bishop asked.

"They're old tables," Ans said, patting the one in front of him, "but these things are *solid.*"

Faye popped the wine and poured.

"What's the deal with Red Raven?" Bishop asked.

Jewel started to answer, then turned to Ans. "You want to tell him? Obviously you remember."

"Jewel had to go to Kansas for a cousin's wedding last year. The night before, there was a kind of bridesmaids' dinner, instead of a bachelorette party—"

"What a rip off," Faye said.

"I know, right?" Jewel said with a snort. "And you better believe her groom had his bachelor party." Then she turned a fond smile on Ans. "But do continue."

"For dinner they had steak, and with it they ordered wine for everyone. Even Jewel. First wine she ever had, and she loved it. A Red Raven pinot noir."

"A story I told you exactly once," Jewel said, shaking her head.

"Stories are the best part of life," Ans said.

"Speaking of stories," Bishop said.

"Ah, ah," Ans said. "First a toast."

They all raised their glasses.

"To us," he said simply, and they all drank.

4

———

OCTOBER 30TH, 8:57 PM.

York was a tricky bastard. Sorenson had to give him that much.

Down the street from Colver High, and around the corner. Sorenson knew better than to park right in front of the old high school, but he never would have guessed that for a parking spot. Never would have figured York would make the girls walk that far.

Hell, Cruiser and the boys had had him half-convinced that York and Magellan had come to their senses and taken their girls somewhere else.

Almost talked Sorenson into skipping out on Colver and crashing that party they passed. The one all lit up like fucking Christmas, with its stupid 80s music blaring to the four winds.

But Cruiser and the boys, they hadn't heard those four in the parking lot. They hadn't heard how excited Magellan had sounded when he proposed Colver High.

No. Those two had something special planned. Sorenson had been sure of it.

That was why he'd gone just a little farther. Looked just a little harder.

And he was right.

Sure enough, there was that lame-ass Charger. Right down the block from that loud party, like York knew the party would distract the cops from noticing any strange cars on the block.

Pretty smart.

Well, two could play at that game.

So Sorenson had parked right next to that fucking Charger. And he and the boys grabbed their loaded backpacks, and all four of them started hoofing it.

No costumes yet, of course. No. Didn't want to risk getting spotted in them until Sorenson was good and ready to start the games. Right now, all four of them were in black.

Jimmy "Grinder" Smith had wanted to wear balaclavas, but that would have been stupid. All in black was one thing. Put on the balaclava and you might as well be waving a sign that says, "Doing something bad!"

A nosy neighbor might keep an eye on four teens in black walking down the street, but turn away as soon as it became clear they weren't heading to *his* house.

Put on balaclavas and that neighbor just assumes they're burglars and calls the cops.

For a point guard, Grinder wasn't all that smart. He was one of those white kids who tried to dress and act like the rap stars — practically modeled himself on Cypress Hill — and Sorenson thought all the pot smoking was probably getting to him.

Sorenson never touched pot, much less anything harder. Booze was fine, of course. Built character. But drugs, man, those were the quick way to a busted career.

Grinder, he might have the skills on the court to net himself a scholarship, but he'd have trouble making grades and sticking to discipline at any college program worth playing for. And he'd never be able to handle the game plans of an NBA team.

But for one more year, he was a good enough soldier. He could follow Sorenson's orders as well as Hector "Cruiser" Rodriguez —

who was a damn fine shooting guard — and Bobby Beef, who played center, but really ought to have been a power forward.

Jamal was the reason Bobby Beef didn't play power forward. Played the low post like he was born to it, and had a fifteen-foot-jumper that made the scouts drool.

But fuck Jamal. Staying at the dance with his girlfriend, when he should have been here helping. Guy had no team spirit.

Fortunately, Cruiser had enough team spirit to pick up the slack. Cruiser was a skinny guy, with that slick, Colombian vibe to his speech. Had to have gotten it from his dad, because his mom was even more white bread than Sorenson. That little lilt to his speech, though. It helped Cruiser play the "Latin lover" game with the ladies. Got him his nickname.

Cruiser also insisted on wearing that lame-ass, pencil-thin black mustache, but whatever.

Robert "Bobby Beef" Nagy had only been in the States for ... oh, not quite a year. Was still working on his English. Speaking it, anyway. Seemed to understand it all right. His whole family spoke Hungarian at home, though, including all three sisters and two other brothers. So he only really got to practice speaking English at school.

Bobby was big and tough. He could have set a pick for a Mack truck and put the truck in the emergency room. Plus, he had a pretty sweet post-up game himself.

Yeah, Bobby Beef was going places too. Once he got his English down.

Had this jagged scar on his face from back home, though. Along the left side of his jaw. But he never talked about how he got it, and the couple of times Sorenson had asked were the only times Bobby stopped smiling.

Sorenson, of course, was a small forward who could do it all. Drive the paint, hit the three, drop dimes, crash the boards. Just like LeBron. And he ran his team the way LeBron ran *his*. A tight ship.

Sorenson knew where the gap in Colver's fence was, of course. The little grove of trees was a good place to hide from his old man, back when Sorenson was small enough to worry about his old man's benders.

That was years ago now. These days, Daddy Sorenson knew better than to raise his fists in anger, though he drank even heavier these days.

But Sorenson figured he still knew Colver's grounds as well as anyone.

Getting Bobby Beef through that gap in the fence wasn't easy. Tore his black shirt, but nothing could be done about that. And Bobby knew better than to bitch about it, where anyone could hear them.

But it left him in a mean mood, and that was good for what Sorenson had in mind.

Into the trees they went, following Sorenson's flashlight beam.

Didn't get halfway to that clearing when he heard someone say, "Busy place tonight, man."

Sorenson stopped dead. Looked right. Saw the cherry and smelled the herb.

Stoners.

No. Not tonight. No randos were going to fuck up Sorenson's plans tonight.

"Seen some others, have you?" Sorenson said, his voice that nasty kind of quiet. Should have shut the guy up. Made his balls crawl up into his body.

If the guy had any sense, he'd have grabbed his friends and vamoosed before Sorenson said anything else.

But the guy must not have had any sense.

"Yeah," he said, like he was sharing a joke with Sorenson. "Couple of guys with a couple of megawatt hotties came through a little bit ago. Hey, Rico, how long you figure?"

"Twenty. Maybe thirty."

"Yeah, maybe half an hour ago. We were just about to go spy on the clearing. Hope we could catch a little of the show, you know? Want to come with?"

Sorenson gave the stoner a look that was probably wasted in the darkness of the woods. Hell, the guy could probably only tell where Sorenson was because of his flashlight.

Sorenson hit the guy with that flashlight beam. Made him shield his eyes, but gave Sorenson a good look. Tubby, unshaven, waste-of-space type.

A quick flick of the wrist told Sorenson that all these stoners fit the same mold.

"No," he said finally. "And I don't want you to do it either. Get me?"

"Hey, man," the stoner said, "it's a free country. They want to share their love out here under the stars, only fair that we catch a peep too. And oh, those looked like two lovelies worth *peeping.*"

"Why don't you and your loser crew get out of here?"

The tone should have been enough. Hell, Sorenson's tone was enough that his boys all dropped their backpacks, ready to throw down.

But man, these stoners were cruising for it.

"Naw, man, you need to mellow out. Come smoke some. We'll give those four a few more to get good and going. Can't even hear 'em yet, so they're probably still all dressed anyway. But, man, when the clothes come off, I want to *see.*"

"Little Red Riding Hood," the other stoner — Rico — said, like he was beckoning Faye. "Big Bad Wolf. I've got a basket of goodies for you, and enough to *share.*"

The lead stoner chuckled, and that was all Sorenson was going to stand for. The thought of a loser like York getting his hands on Faye's sweet body was bad enough, but the idea of these assholes *watching*? Of sneaking peeks at *Faye*?

Oh, no. No fucking way.

"Last warning," Sorenson said. "Clear off or die."

That made the stoner look at him. Really look at him. As though even after getting splashed with the flashlight beam he had good enough night vision to really see the look on Sorenson's face. But Sorenson could never see shit in the dark, so he figured "night vision" was pretty much an urban legend.

"Yeah," the stoner said, nodding. "All right, man. We'll do that. Just as soon as we finish our joint. No skin off our nose. Can always head back to Rico's place and watch Skinemax anyway."

"Nah," Rico said. "They cut us off. Have to stream something."

"Good enough."

While the stoners were talking, Cruiser leaned in and spoke softly to Sorenson.

"Man, you want to risk those guys changing their mind and catching a look at what *we* do here?"

Sorenson shook his head. Cleared his throat.

And that was all it took to get his boys in motion.

There were six stoners, but they'd been at their pot, their beer and their snacks for hours.

Hell, even if they'd been ready and cruising for it, they probably couldn't have handled Sorenson and his boys. Especially not with Bobby Beef already pissed about his shirt.

As it was, the whole beat-down didn't take thirty seconds. Hardly enough to build up a sweat.

But spilling a little blood, that was always good to get the juices flowing. And it would make their war paint look all that much better, when it came time to costume up.

Plus, watching those beaten-down stoners crawl for the fences, all teary and bloody, that just made Sorenson feel good. They deserved it for talking about Faye that way.

Yeah. This was just was Sorenson and his boys needed. A little scrimmage before the game.

...BLOOD.

Blood.

Blood.

BLOOD!

Blood spilled on the ground. Into the ground, like a lover's seed.

Blood was memory. Blood was life. Blood was...

Blood was right.

Blood was *necessary*.

Yes. They remembered blood. They did. They remembered much and more of blood. And pain. And death.

They remembered things that They had forgotten for time untold. No way to tell.

Not here.

This place. This bound place. These borders They could not cross. Those boundaries that kept Them tied down. Kept Them from rising up again. Kept Them from so much unspent blood.

The natives had kept Them bound here, with their shamans and their medicines. Until the natives were driven away.

The Chinese had kept Them bound here, with their spells and their alchemy. Until the white man spent their blood and made a mound of their bones.

Then the Chinese left too.

The white priests came next. The priests had kept Them bound here, with their incense and their prayers, until the priests were forced to sell the land.

Then turmoil. Construction. Deaths and blood, hidden behind accidents. Enough for a time.

Then the children came. The glorious year the children came. The children came with their dreams and their lives and their unspent blood.

The children went unnoticed for a time, so sated were They on blood and death from the construction.

But with time, They stirred once more. With time, They were ready.

Oh, how the children and their keepers bled on that sweet day. Oh, how many of them fell that last time. Too much and too many for patience. Too much and too many for pretense.

But glorious, glorious blood.

How long ago?

Uncertain. All fell then.

Enough to sustain for years. Decades. More?

The next time They awoke, They were bound once more.

Someone else had come, while They slept. Someone whose blood knew things. Someone who bound Them all once more into the ground. With salt and blood and magic. Bound Them here, and kept Them bound.

They had slept, and waited. Those few times They roused, They tore impotently at Their bonds, before falling into torpor once more.

But now *blood* had been spilled again.

Little blood, true, but blood spilled by *violence*.

The sweetest blood.

Oh, how it dripped down into the ground. Oh, how welcome. How *needed*.

Perfect blood. Exactly what They needed to loosen the bonds.

Blood spilled just right. Blood spilled with intention. Blood spilled with joy.

Not for *safety*. Not to defend.

Blood spilled to *dominate*. Blood spilled for *pleasure*.

And now, now They rustled once more.

Strengthened by that blood, They pressed against Their bonds.

They pushed and pushed and *pushed*.

Not yet.

But They would continue. They would worry at Their chains.

Soon They would break these bonds.

Soon They would be free.

Soon. Oh, soon, there would be *blood*.

Glorious blood.

Blood?

A wave of cold fear washed over Faye that had nothing to do with the spooky story Ans was telling.

He'd been in the middle of a good one. Leaning over a candle and relating the story as much with his hands and expressions as with his words. It was a tale about a fisherman in Half Moon Bay, and a light-house, and this *thing* that came out of the sea one night.

This was the best way to have scary storytelling, far as Faye was concerned. A creepy — yet comfortable enough — little place to themselves. The four of them sitting on those nice sleeping bags. Sharing the sweet, dry taste of a Red Raven pinot noir and savoring the way it went with cheese and chocolates.

Especially the creamy dark chocolate she'd just enjoyed.

Faye had been happily snuggled up against Bishop, with his warmth and his strong arms and his good, manly scent. Sinking into Ans' tale, and worrying about the fisherman, and whether or not he would live to see the dawn—

That was when the cold wave of fear hit her. Like ice water over her face. Down her spine. Settling in her gut.

Turned her skin to gooseflesh. Pulled in her arms and legs so tight her shivering was an afterthought.

Bishop kissed her neck like he thought she was reacting to the story. His lips fever-hot against her now-clammy skin. Almost burning.

Barely noticed.

Faye could feel ... she wasn't sure what she felt. That was the damnable shame of it.

Her grandmother had told her all about these feelings, these moments, these intuitions, back when Faye was a girl.

All Conroy women have a touch of the Sight, Nanna Conroy had said. *It comes and goes, and it won't always make sense. But when it comes you always trust it, my little Faye child. Always.*

"Won't always make sense" was right though. All Faye knew, in that fleeting moment of intuition, was fear. The sense of danger. Of blood. Of something ... malevolent.

But was it a threat here and now? Was it something that happened here a long time ago? There were those scratches on that one door. The ones that looked like a huge dog had desperately tried to get inside.

And behind that door ... something bad had happened.

Faye knew that for certain.

But this ... this felt different. Still, two intuitions in one night. What were the—

"Hello?" Ans said, waving his hand in front of her. "Earth to Faye."

Bishop's chuckle rumbled low against her back, but Faye wasn't relaxed enough to enjoy the sensation.

"Story get to you?" he asked, that teasing way of his. Inviting her to object. Inviting her to outdo his friend. Ready to reward her if she could.

That was his way, and she loved him for it.

But Jewel, Jewel had that suspicious look in her eyes. Which meant she knew Faye was having what she referred to as "one of her fits."

Faye should never have told Jewel about what Nanna Conroy had told her. But they were best friends. Shared everything. She'd had no idea Jewel would take such a ... religious spin on it.

To Jewel, Faye's intuitions were either bullshit or the devil's work. Even the time Faye's sudden need to slow down and change lanes had helped them avoid both a speed trap *and* an accident at the same time, Jewel still didn't believe a word of it.

"Wasn't the story," Ans said. "She didn't even react to the big twist. You all right, Faye?"

Ans looked confused. Maybe hurt that she'd drifted away.

"I'm sorry, Ans," Faye said. Or tried to say. It came out more of a, "Uh suh."

She tried to clear her throat and start again, but Jewel overrode her.

"You were just in the moment," Jewel said. "*Weren't you, Faye?*"

Faye couldn't answer the intensity in Jewel's eyes. Not right away. That intuition had been so *strong*. But was it a threat?

Or was it like the time she'd been terrified by a motel room that turned out to have once been the site of a triple-homicide?

She sipped her wine to buy time. She could practically *feel* Bishop's curious concern. Ans' confusion. Worst of all, Jewel's disapproval.

Jewel would kill her if she asked to leave and ruined all Ans' hard work, setting this up.

It was probably just an echo of the past, reaching out to scare her.

"Yeah, I was in the moment," Faye said. "I was thinking about the lighthouse cat. What would happen to poor little First Mate, after, you know, the fisherman..."

"*Oh*," Ans said, mollified. "Well, don't worry. There's a little coda all about the cat that will make you feel better then."

Jewel's penetrating stare lingered a moment, but she gave a little nod. As though this answer was good enough. She turned back to Ans.

Faye snuggled back into Bishop's arms.

"You're half frozen," he whispered.

"So hold me tight," she answered. "Warm me up."

He did, and Faye tried to convince herself that that was all she needed.

SORENSON WASN'T SURPRISED WHEN HE DIDN'T FIND FAYE AND THE others in that little clearing in the grove of long pines. Cruiser and the boys could make all the disappointed sounds they wanted to.

Sorenson knew better.

Faye. He'd never figured her for the kind of girl who'd be willing to get naked and go to town where any stupid old stoner might catch a free show.

For that matter, he'd never figured Jewel Girard for that kind either.

No, those two had more class than that. Even if York and Magellan didn't.

The clearing was only worth checking in case York and Magellan had been stupid enough to bring them there and try something. But from the look of the clearing, they hadn't done that either.

Sure, there were some bent patches of grass that implied *some-*

body'd gotten laid out here tonight, but no way was it Faye. Wasn't recent enough, and from the look of things, it was only one couple.

Still. Deep down inside, something in Sorenson relaxed when he didn't find Faye there. Like maybe part of him had wondered.

But no. That was stupid. She couldn't have gotten *that* wild. This was the girl who'd barely been willing to give him a good night kiss on their third and final date.

Yeah, she'd changed since then, for sure. Grown. They both had. She'd see that, how Sorenson had grown up. How he'd changed. How he'd become the right man for her.

He just needed to get her to look at York differently. To see him for the loser coward waste-of-space that he was.

Of course, to do that, he'd have to find them. And since Faye and the others *weren't* in the clearing, his boys were getting a little impatient.

They'd had a taste of blood, and they wanted more action.

Well, a leader knew how to handle that.

Sorenson started laughing.

That distracted the others from peering into the trees with their flashlights, as though they might spot York and Magellan, hiding half-naked behind a long pine.

"You guys don't get it, do you?" Sorenson shook his head. "Look, even a loser like York knows you don't impress a babe like Faye by bringing her *here*." He pointed at the grass under their feet. "You impress her by bringing her *there*."

He pointed through the trees at the huge goddamn wart-topped box that once was Colver High.

"You really think they found a way in?" Grinder asked.

Sorenson nodded. "It's perfect. They found a way in, and they think they're the only ones who know about it. All we have to do is find their entrance, and we can set up everything we need."

And with that, he turned and started for the main building. Sorenson didn't need to look over his shoulder. He knew the others would fall into line.

They did, hurrying to catch up.

He led them straight up to the front steps. That was the primary entrance, so it seemed the most likely.

But he barely bothered checking the doors.

They'd had glass panels once, but even the chicken wire hadn't been enough. Somewhere along the way, those panels had been knocked out, and thick-sounding wooden boards hammered over the gaps, from the inside. The door handles were locked with thick chains, and those same tough fucking padlocks Sorenson remembered from his last try. With the hammer.

All the same, he pushed and pulled. Just in case. He tested the panels, and the area around the door.

While the others stood there staring, like useless benchwarmers.

"Check the windows." He shook his head. Did LeBron have to micromanage like this?

"Can't reach," Grinder said.

"Then stand on Bobby's shoulders. What, do I have to think of everything?"

"What good's that?" Cruiser asked, whispering so the other two wouldn't hear. "No way they got in through those windows. Not without a ladder, and I don't see one."

"I know," Sorenson said, watching the other two stumble around in their attempt to get at the closest windows. "They just piss me off sometimes. I shouldn't have to think of everything, you know?"

"Heavy hangs the head," Cruiser said, and Sorenson shoved him.

"Come on," Sorenson said, just as Bobby and Grinder were almost at a window. "Let's check the other two sets of doors first."

Turned out, they only needed to check one set of doors.

They got to the south side, and lo and behold, no chain on the door.

Sorenson smiled at Cruiser, then the others.

"Told you," he crowed. "I knew they'd found a way in."

He called them into a huddle.

"All right." Sorenson tapped Cruiser on the chest. "You're the sneakiest. You slip in and find where they've got their little make-out session going. Then come back and report."

He grabbed Cruiser's collar. "Recon only, got me? Don't do anything stupid."

Cruiser nodded.

Sorenson let go. Reached out and tapped Bobby, Grinder, and himself on the chest. "The three of us will start getting ready." He tapped Cruiser again. "You too, after you get back and report."

"Then what?" Grinder asked in a hushed whisper.

"Then," Sorenson said. "Then the fun begins."

5

OCTOBER 30TH, 9:21 PM.

Bishop had to hand it to Jewel. She was a pretty good storyteller.

Ans had been a hard act to follow, with his fisherman story. He'd clearly been rehearsing it for weeks. No surprise, given how much work he'd put into tonight. Probably wouldn't even need to read his second story of the night from his phone or a printout, like the rest of them would.

No, Ans probably had his second story rehearsed and ready to go.

That thought made Bishop smile. Ans didn't show him up very often. It'd be good for Ans to do that once in a while. Remind *himself* that he and Bishop were equal partners in this friendship.

But Jewel, she was outdoing herself tonight. Last year, her weird little camping-slasher story, that hadn't been very good.

Oh, Bishop would never have admitted that out loud. Faye would never have forgiven him. Jewel had been trying her best.

Still, she must have known she fell short. Because this time, she was *really* into it.

Hers was a ghost story, set in a bed and breakfast in a little town on the coast, just down the freeway from Monterey. The haunting had to do with an outlaw on the run from Civil War crimes, an innkeeper's daughter, and a Federal marshal.

Bishop suspected it would have as much of a romantic ending as a spooky ending, but that was all right. The romantic ones always made Faye cuddlier.

Though she'd been practically wrapping herself in Bishop ever since the end of Ans' story. Almost felt as though she'd have crawled inside Bishop's body, if she could have.

Something must have gotten to her. If not the story, maybe the setting. Bishop wasn't sure.

He did know that she'd barely touched her wine since then.

Well, Bishop didn't blame her for that. He'd managed to down half a cup, but this pinot noir was really not his thing. He would much rather have had some tequila. Or maybe vodka. Or some good old fashioned beer.

But wine was what Ans supplied, and clearly it was a gift for Jewel.

Still, Ans could have warned Bishop. Maybe brought a back-up drink for him.

Didn't matter. This was still the place to be. Even if they *had* gotten kicked out of the dance too soon. This old teachers' lounge was big, but warming up with the four of them sitting around the two, low coffee tables. And the flannel inside of the sleeping bag underneath him and Faye was doing its job of retaining heat and giving it back to them.

Place felt downright comfortable. And with the smell of the air freshener, and the taste of the dark chocolates, this hardly felt like an abandoned school at all.

Everything was right, to let Bishop really sink into Jewel's story. The young couple at the bed and breakfast were just finding out about the Civil War gold the outlaw had stolen, and the trail leading to the caves down near the shore...

Wait. What was that?

"Hush a second," Bishop said, raising one hand and looking up. He'd have sworn he heard footsteps up above him.

Jewel frowned, but stalled her storytelling when Ans put his hand on her wrist.

"What, Bish?" Ans asked, quiet.

"Footsteps, I think."

"It wasn't footsteps," Faye said, which made Jewel frown deeper.

But then he heard the sound again. Soft, at first, barely there. A low kind of beating sound.

Bishop closed his eyes. Strained his ears.

Yes. There it was.

Thump thump thump thump. *Thump* thump thump thump.

Regular rhythm. Repeating.

Then the sound got louder.

"I hear it," Ans said. Jewel nodded and Bishop felt Faye nod against his chest.

"Drums?" Ans asked.

"Yeah," Bishop said.

"Isn't that the sound of native drumming in like, every cowboy movie ever made?"

That question was from Jewel.

Bishop only nodded.

Then the drumming got louder. And it didn't just come from above them. It came from all around them—

"It's everywhere," Ans whispered.

Bishop and the others got to their feet.

"No," Bishop said. "Above us." He pointed to the walls separating the lounge from the rooms on either side. "And those two rooms."

"That's right," Faye said, frowning as she looked around. There was something off about Faye's expression. As though she were almost expecting something like this.

"Should we check it out?" Ans asked.

Bishop nodded. "You and me."

He turned to Faye, who gave him one of her eyebrow-raised, take-no-bullshit looks.

"Excuse *me*," she said. "If you think you two he-men are going to go out there and leave us behind like scared little girls—"

"Yeah," Jewel said. "One of us goes, we're *all* going."

"Fine," Bishop said. "But I'll take point. Ans, you cover the rear."

"That's more like it," Faye said, and the four of them fell into formation.

Bishop led them to the door of the room. All four with their LED flashlights in hand and on.

Was the drumming getting louder? More complicated with a second rhythm?

No. That was just his heartbeat, getting involved. Bishop could practically taste his rapid pulse.

He ripped open the door—

Nothing. Just an empty hallway.

No. Wait.

He tracked along the hallway with his flashlight beam.

There. Tacked to the wall directly opposite their room. A white sign, with red lettering.

Paleface die tonight

"What the fuck?" Bishop said, his words echoing loudly in the hallway.

"Someone's in here with us," Faye said.

"Sorenson?" Bishop didn't try to keep the anger out of his voice. Bastard had already ruined the dance. Was he trying to ruin Devil's Night storytelling too?

"I hope so," Faye said. "Because the alternative is someone we don't know."

"What is it?" Jewel asked, and Bishop and Faye had to go into the hallway, so Jewel and Ans could come forward and see.

"Got to be Sorenson," Jewel said. "It's his level of mentality."

"Drumming's definitely coming from those two rooms," Ans said, gesturing with his flashlight to the rooms on the sides of their lounge.

"And up above," Bishop said, panning up. "Pretty sure I hear it coming from there."

Faye nodded agreement.

"Let's check the upstairs first," Ans said, quietly now. "They'll be expecting us to check the close rooms. Probably Sorenson in there with his cronies, ready to jump out and yell, 'Boo!'"

Jewel nodded. Ans locked the door of the lounge, but before they took a step down the hall, Bishop stopped him.

"Where'd you get *that* key?"

Ans grinned. "It was hanging on a hook in the room, first time I came in. Figured it would come in handy."

"Yeah," Jewel said, giving Ans a squeeze. "Don't want that bastard drinking our wine or eating our cheese and chocolates."

"Which way are the stairs?" Bishop, said, dropping his already-low tone to a whisper.

"I'll lead," Ans said, and took point, Jewel behind him, then Faye, then Bishop.

They passed the next room along the hall. All four of them creeping as quietly as they could, although none of them were wearing the stealthiest of shoes. Bishop and Ans had on nice black loafers to go with the zoot suits, Faye's were low black boots, and Jewel had on low things that were probably boots, but were covered in wolf fur halfway to the knee.

They got maybe five steps past the door to the next room when someone flung it open, bellowing a wordless war cry.

Bishop reacted without thinking.

"Run!" he yelled.

All four of them blitzed their way down the hardwood of the hallway. Kicking up dust all around them. Stamping old bits of detritus. Ans may have swept their entry, but they were off Ans' map now.

A glance behind. Two chasers.

Bishop's beam caught ghost-white skin. Buckskin loincloths. Tomahawks trailing feathers. Headdresses with more feathers.

Red streaks like blood on their cheeks.

And they were gaining.

ANS WASN'T A SPRINTER UNDER THE BEST CONDITIONS. EVEN IF YOU gave him a track and a sunny day and a real professional helping him stretch out, he'd still lose a race to more than half the school.

And he sure as hell wasn't built to run full out down a dusty old hallway with someone on his heels.

His feet ached in his loafers. Probably already had blisters forming. His lungs pumped faster than his arms, and his heart pounded faster still. All that cheese in his gut like an anchor, slowing every stride.

Why did muenster have to be so tasty?

Worse still was the dust. Itching his nose. Almost choking him with the need to cough.

His legs already burned from the effort.

And they'd barely run two rooms.

Jewel already caught him. Her long legs matching him stride for stride. Pushing him to run faster.

The stairs! Only steps away!

The stairs were all concrete. Wider at the bottom but tapering quickly on their way up.

Ans grabbed for the wooden rail. Tried to use it to deftly turn. Use his momentum to propel himself up the stairs.

Didn't work. His hand slipped right off.

He tumbled across the hard concrete and slammed into the other side. Sharp pains through his shins, his hands, his arms. Shoulders, too. Only just lucky he ducked his head in time, or he'd've been out cold for sure.

Dropped his flashlight somewhere in there though.

"Help him!" Bishop's voice.

Crap, was that his hero tone? Was he doing something stupid?

Jewel there. Faye too. Each grabbed a shoulder. Tried to pull him up, but the hallway was spinning and he had trouble getting his feet under him.

"I need a sec."

"We don't have it!" Jewel said.

A sound. Wind through a knothole?

No. More like someone going "woo!" loud and long, while rapidly slapping their hand over their mouth to break the sound.

Someone was waiting on the stairs above them.

———

BISHOP SAW ANS GO DOWN. LOOKED LIKE A BAD SPILL. BAD ENOUGH that Ans might be done running.

"Help him!" he yelled. Then he turned right there in the hallway. Terrible place to fight, when he was outnumbered. The hallway was wide enough that the two chasing him could flank him.

Plus, he was wearing these stupid loafers. Great for dancing. Lousy for anything like footwork on an old, dusty hardwood floor.

But Bishop could do one thing to help himself.

He widened his flashlight beam and hit the "ghosts" full in the face. They shouted and stumbled to a stop like people, not spirits from the beyond.

Now was the time. He had a moment. Just a moment, and it might not last. Before they got their bearings.

Now was the time to strike. To punch. Kick. Go for the nuts. Take them out before they could raise those things that looked like tomahawks.

But Bishop's dad always told him, "York men don't start fights. We finish them."

And so far, this wasn't a fight. It was a prank.

These two had given him a good scare. Sure. Startled him with their cry and their ghostly look.

But they didn't look so much like ghosts, now that Bishop could stop and take a second. Their pallor was clown makeup. Their costumes, cheap. Bishop had seen those outfits at Ghosts and Gaffs, on the clearance rack. Mocked them for being archaic and insulting.

The tomahawks didn't look like steel now. Hard rubber maybe.

And the two guys carrying them could only be Robert Nagy and Hector Rodriguez.

Another stereotypical native call, from somewhere behind him. That tremolo "woo" from old cowboy movies.

Had to be Sorenson...

No.

Bishop would have to leave Sorenson for the others right now. He didn't dare turn his back on these two.

"Lower that fucking light, asshole." Yep. Rodriguez. Bishop recognized the voice.

"Got a lot of nerve calling *me* asshole after a stunt like that."

"You *are* asshole, *asshole*," Nagy said, straightening up to his impressive height and bulk, which were more than enough to make Bishop decide that fighting was definitely not his best option.

They called that guy Bobby Beef for a reason.

"All right," Bishop said, lowering the beam from their faces, but keeping it only a twitch away from blinding them again. He held up his other hand in what he hoped was a reassuring fashion. "You gave us a turn. I don't deny it. Good prank. Now clear out, huh?"

But Nagy and Rodriguez just grinned and shook their heads.

"White man trespass." Sorenson's voice, from somewhere behind Bishop. On the stairs maybe? "Must pay price."

"You *racist* motherfucker," Jewel said.

"*John Sorenson.*" Faye's voice, and Bishop found himself devoutly hoping she never turned a tone that icy on *him*. Deep space had to be warmer than that tone.

"This is the lowest," Faye continued, and Bishop felt sure that her words alone were dropping the ambient temperature. "The most *despicable* thing you have *ever* done. And with you, that's saying something."

"Faye?" Sorenson said, all pretense of his game gone now. "No! Wait! You don't understand—"

"Understand *what*? That you don't respect me enough to *listen* when I say no? That you aren't man enough to—"

"You aren't supposed to *be* here! You're supposed to be—"

"Cowering like a little girl? Waiting for the great *John Sorenson* to come save me?"

"No. I…"

"What's the move, Sore?" Rodriguez yelled out.

"Hold on—" Sorenson said, but Bishop missed the rest of whatever he said, because Nagy rumbled out something more important.

"Enough talk."

Nagy might not have been seven feet tall, but he was close enough to split the difference. And with his build, he must have weighed close to three hundred pounds.

And all of it was coming right at Bishop.

He tried blinding Nagy with his flashlight beam, but Nagy was ready. Ducked his head. Squinted his eyes. Maybe closed them. Bishop wasn't waiting to find out.

Bishop jumped right. Tried to get out of the way of the charging bull.

No good. Nagy flung his fists out to the side, stretching his arms wide and hooking Bishop's ribs.

Nagy pulled him in tight. Arms as big as Bishop's legs squeezed his ribs so tight he couldn't breathe. He could feel his face going red. His blood pounding in his head.

He tried to swing back his elbows. Go for Nagy's ribs, but he couldn't get past those arms. Tried for the head, but Nagy had his head ducked.

Then the blows to Bishop's stomach began.

Fast, tight punches, thrown by someone who knew what he was doing. Bishop couldn't see more than some shadows and grays — he'd dropped his flashlight — but it had to be Rodriguez.

The world was already going black on Bishop from lack of air. Add in the pain in his ribs and the series of pains in his guts, all the fight was draining out of him quickly.

He managed one good kick. He was going for Rodriguez's balls, but he caught him too high. The stomach. Must have been higher off the ground in Nagy's arms than he thought.

The contact of that kick felt good. The only thing that did. His head was jackhammering and his ribs felt like they were breaking and he couldn't breathe, and his guts were screaming at him.

The last thing Bishop heard before he lost consciousness was Rodriguez swearing in Spanish.

THESE GUYS REALLY WERE PLAYING THE NATIVE GHOST THING TO THE hilt. Sorenson and Smith stood just below the first landing. Fake buckskin loincloths, clown white all over their bodies, moccasins. Even hard rubber tomahawks and feathered headdresses — one feather at the back for Smith, and a full headdress dripping down over the shoulders for Sorenson.

That "warpaint" on their cheeks looked more like dried blood than red paint. Disturbing.

Right now, the jerks' attention was on Faye and Jewel. Mostly on Faye, though. She berated Sorenson like he'd had this coming for two years and had finally pushed things too far.

"You aren't a third the man Bishop is! You're..."

For her part, though, Jewel was giving it pretty good too.

"Lowlife, scum-sucking piece of shit wannabe Lebron..."

Entertaining as the barrage of insults were, Ans kept his focus on himself.

While the tirade was going on, he managed to get his feet under himself on the stairs. Unfortunately, that was about all the good news he had. He still hurt almost *everywhere*. His back, ribs, arms, legs. That had been a pretty bad spill.

Still, it was good he could stand on his own — or at least lean against the wall — while Jewel and Faye lit into Sorenson. Every minute they could give him would help him get himself together.

He tried limiting his attention to his breathing. On getting past those pains, in case Sorenson decided to make this physical.

Ans might not be a great fighter, but he was tenacious. If it came to it, he might—

What was that?

Hard to hear over the yelling.

"And another thing—"

Quick steps. A small, rough sound of pain. Little thumps like…
Punches.

"Shit," Ans said. He didn't have his flashlight. Couldn't get a good look though the gloom. Especially with both Faye and Jewel focusing their beams on Sorenson while they lit into him verbally.

"*Bishop!*" Ans yelled, and that was all it took to get through to Faye.

She whirled around. Lit up the scene, but there wasn't much to see now. Nagy was holding Bishop, who dangled unconscious in the big man's arms.

Rodriguez was leaning back against the wall, hands on his belly. He was saying something, but it was soft and Spanish and Ans didn't want to know what it was. His family spoke Portuguese at home sometimes, and that was no help at all with Spanish slang.

He did see hatred for Bishop glaring in Rodriguez's eyes.

The stairwell was suddenly so quiet that Rodriguez' words sounded loud. Despite himself, Ans heard, "*Hijo de puta. Chingata—*"

"Let. Him. Go," Faye said, but whatever power her voice held over Sorenson, it didn't have on Nagy. The big Hungarian just grinned and shook his head.

Sorenson hesitated then. Probably stuck. Poor obsessed bastard wasn't getting the little scene of triumph he'd played out in his head. How he ever thought this would help him win back Faye, Ans couldn't imagine.

Jewel turned away like Sorenson wasn't worth her time. Joined Faye there in the hallway, maybe a step or two from Nagy and Rodriguez. She started yelling at Nagy.

"You heard the lady," Jewel said, so loud now that Ans could barely hear what was going on behind him. "She said to put her *boyfriend* down, and maybe — just maybe — we won't got to the cops about what you assholes have been doing here tonight."

Maybe it was being ignored. Maybe it was mentioning the cops. Or maybe it was some sick and twisted attempt to salvage his efforts, but Sorenson started coming down the stairs. Slow and deliberate. Only just loud enough for Ans to hear his steps.

Ans turned.

But if Sorenson had a flashlight, it wasn't on. And with the girls both focusing their attention on Nagy — both of them yelling at him now — Ans wasn't sure quite where Sorenson was.

Ans started down off the stairs. Wanted to get over to the girls, where he'd at least have *some* safety. He didn't like the way this was playing out.

But Ans, alas, wasn't moving very fast. Not when every step, every movement was hurting. He was starting to think he'd cracked a bone in his left shin. The initial point of contact when he fell. And he had bruises that felt at least that bad in so, so many places.

Someone grabbed him from behind. Hand over his mouth.

Ans tried to bite the fingers that held him, but no good.

Whoever held Ans slammed his head against the hardwood wall to his right.

Bright, fresh pain exploded all through his skull.

And that was all Ans could take. He slipped to the floor. Unconscious.

THIS WAS GOING ALL WRONG.

All. Wrong.

York and Magellan. *They* were the ones who were supposed to come investigate the drumming.

York. And *Magellan.*

The girls, they were supposed to stay in the make-out room and wait. They were supposed to be a little nervous, maybe. All right, scared a little. Maybe remembering all the stories of the Indians here. The cannibals or whatever.

They were supposed to let the *men* go investigate while *they stayed put.* Wasn't that how it was always supposed to be? From caveman times on up?

The men took the risks. The men investigated strange sounds in the dark.

The women *stayed put.* In the *light.* Where they were *safe.*

Damn it. Weren't York and Magellan even men enough to go investigating on their own?

Apparently not.

No, those wusses had to hide behind Faye and Jewel's skirts like scared little boys.

Now everything was fucked up.

Faye took it all wrong. Of course. The way she was yelling. Whuf. *Coach Rutherford* didn't yell this bad after a loss.

But a little yelling, Sorenson could handle. He'd been yelled at all his life. His dad, his mom, his coaches, his teachers. Hell, even Principal Null like to take his turn yelling.

Yelling was no big deal.

Yelling was still talking. Lines of communication were still open, so long as someone was yelling.

And as long as the lines of communication were still open, Sorenson just *knew* he could salvage this.

But first, he had to deal with the troops.

Fucking Cruiser. Couldn't control Bobby Beef. He had one fucking job down there, and he couldn't do it.

Bobby Beef, he should have been easy. No way York was dumb enough to insult someone big as Bobby Beef. All Cruiser had to do was keep York focused on himself, and everything would have stayed on plan.

Or at least, as close as Sorenson could bring it. After those fucking wusses ruined it.

But no. Cruiser had to question him. That opened the door, and Bobby Beef, tough guy that he was, decided to lay a hurt on York.

Sorenson couldn't really blame Bobby for that. Hell, maybe he wanted to hurt York as much as Sorenson did. No telling with Bobby sometimes.

Damn it though. Sorenson had figured *Grinder* would be the edgy one. The one ready to pop at the first sign of an opening.

Fucking Cruiser. He'd pay for this.

Now, Sorenson had to do damage control.

He started down the stairs, while Faye and Jewel were moved on to yelling nasty, *personal* things about Bobby.

Bad idea there. They should have stuck to threatening him with the cops. Wouldn't have *worked*, but it wouldn't have pissed him off any more than he already was.

Must have been frustrated that the other insults they'd lobbed weren't getting the results they wanted. Sorenson could relate. Bobby Beef could be stubborn as a bull.

See, that was just it. Sorenson *could* relate to what she was going through. He and Faye would have so much in common, if only...

One thing at a time.

Magellan was still up. That was no good. He'd taken a pretty good fall though. Probably couldn't take much more...

Sorenson swept the little prick up in both hands at the same time. One around his mouth, and one slamming his head into the wall. Hard. Twice.

Sorenson dropped Magellan. Smacked Grinder in the chest and shoved him at the fallen wuss.

Even Grinder was smart enough to know that meant to grab the prick.

Sorenson reached the bottom of the stairs around the time Faye had gotten back around to legal threats.

"...and you won't see the light of day again. I swear it. Both my parents are attorneys, and they love Bishop almost as much as I do. You will be behind bars for the rest of your unnatural bovine—"

Sorenson cleared his throat.

"—life. You'll be chewing your cud all by yourself. And you'll never get near a basketball again."

"Faye," Sorenson tried. But she kept going.

"Unless you count the prison team. But there'll be bigger guys than you there. And they'll turn you from Bobby Beef into Bobby Bitch. Now you *let. Him. Go.*"

Damn it.

Even now, Faye wasn't giving Sorenson the time of day. Even *unconscious*, York was commanding all of Faye's attention.

Even now, she was just fucking *ignoring* Sorenson.

Well fuck it then. He'd been ignored long enough.

"Shut the fuck up!" he yelled, and with all the practice yelling he got during games and running plays, he could get plenty of volume out of his voice when he wanted to.

Faye turned so slowly, he thought she might have actually *heard* him for once.

"What did you just say?"

There was that tone again. There was that fucking stuck-up, holier-than-thou tone she'd been giving since she'd called out Sorenson's full name like she was his fucking mother or something.

"I'll get to you," Sorenson said.

"What did you—" Jewel was trying to back up Faye, same as always.

Well, Sorenson had even less patience for *her* bullshit here and now.

"No!" he yelled to cut her off. Then just said, "Cruiser."

Cruiser grabbed her arms. Jewel started to struggle.

"Just what do you think you're doing?" Faye asked.

"What I should have done in the first place," Sorenson said. "What I should have done two years ago."

He leaned in a little closer.

"I'm taking charge, bitch. You *will* hear me out. And when you do, you *will* see that I'm the guy for you, and not that puss-nuts, wimp of boyfriend you seem to think the world of."

He looked at Bobby Beef and nodded.

"You can't possibly think—"

Faye didn't get to finish that sentence. Bobby Beef dropped York and grabbed her. One arm around her arms. One hand over her mouth.

Yes. Sorenson was taking charge now. And he was going to make everything the way he wanted it.

Blood.

Yes. More blood spilled. They could smell it. They could almost taste it.

Sweet, sweet blood.

Blood spilled *inside the dead tree place.*

Not much. But *inside.*

Some blood outside. Among the live trees, but inside the perimeter. Out where the tougher bonds were. Out where the living taunted Them. Came to sit, as though knowing They waited close enough to rend and tear and rip.

But not able to do so.

But that little bit of blood spilled among the trees. Just a taste, but a beginning. Just a smidge, but enough to rouse Them. To set Them to testing their bonds once more.

But the bonds had not been loosened enough. That little bit of blood spilled among the trees, its power would fade before They could shed their bonds. By dawn it would be gone completely.

But now. Oh, now.

Now blood *inside.* Inside the dead tree place. Inside the second layer of bondage.

Oh, how They shivered at the realization.

Oh, how They stretched and strained at Their bonds, desperate for the blood.

Twice in one night. Twice before the same dawn.

Blood spilled *twice.*

Once outside among the living trees. Once inside the dead tree structure.

No accidents here.

No, no, no. Twice blood not dripped, but *spilled.* By *violence.* Done with *spite,* with *malice,* with *deliberation,* with *pleasure.*

Yes. Oh, yes.

The blood, it seeped into the dead tree structure. Inside the innermost bonds.

They stretched. They strained.

Oh, how They pressed at the magics that held Them trapped.

Not. Yet. Enough.

Curse the woman who knew the old ways. Whose blood sang with more power than even the priests had called down to bind Them.

Blood spilled twice in one night. But even twice was not enough. Not yet.

Oh, the blood would still reach Them. The blood spilled on the dead wood, it would seep into the air. It would sink down within.

Soon. Oh, so soon. Soon They would connect with that blood. Taste it. Revel in it.

Soon They would loosen Their bonds further.

But They knew the laws. They knew more about the ancient powers than any human ever could.

Which was why, in the end, They would always triumph.

Twice was not enough.

But three times. Oh, yes. Three times. *That* would be enough.

Seven would be perfect. Seven would free them from all bonds entirely. Seven spills of blood by human violence, if done with the right intention.

Glorious enough that They might even grant a boon to a human willing to spill blood seven times for Them.

Too much to ask. If that were to happen, it would have happened before now.

Likely now, no one alive knew to offer Them blood.

Likely now, all had forgotten Them. Save the woman who knew the old ways. And whatever apprentice she took.

Still. All had been silent so long, Their torpor had grown deep. They never expected to be offered fresh blood twice in this one night.

But what can happen twice, can happen *three* times.

Yes. A third time. That was not too much to ask. It might even be *likely*.

A third time. That would be enough for Them to slip their bonds.

Perhaps slip them forever.

So They stretched. And They strained. And They tested those bonds.

But most of all, They waited.

And They knew, deep within Their core, that They would not wait long.

Soon.

6

———

OCTOBER 30TH. TIME UNCERTAIN.

The first clue that Ans had regained consciousness was pain.

Of course, it helped that he had a *lot* of pains.

The worst was his head. To say it pounded didn't do his pain justice. It was more as though some construction company was using massive equipment to drive a series of girders two hundred feet below the surface of his skull.

Every breath. Every beat of his heart. Just *blinking his eyes* seemed to make the pain in his head even worse.

Ans couldn't imagine that he could possibly hurt any more than he did right then.

To make matters worse, the room was kind of ... swimming around Ans. It was taking him a moment to even figure out where he was. What little he could see in the light of someone's flashlight beam.

He used that moment to distract himself from the pain in his head, by cataloging the rest of his pains.

After his skull, the worst source was his left shin. Yeah, he *had* to have cracked that thing. Sharp, fiery pain. It just hurt so damn bad he could almost forget his head for a moment.

Yeah, one shallow breath was enough to keep *that* from happening.

The breath also reminded him that he'd hurt his ribs on the stairs. Not as bad as the shin, but still. Those had to be some winners of bruises.

Other bruises called out from his forearms, his knees, and...

Oh, hell. Damn near the only thing that *didn't* hurt was his groin.

Thank God for small favors.

Once he had those pains cataloged, Ans could expand his awareness enough to realize he was bound. Tied to a chair. His arms behind him, tied to the back of the chair, and his legs tied to chair legs.

He wanted to shake and pull at the ropes, but he didn't. Whoever had tied him up — well, whichever of the gruesome foursome were in here with him — they hadn't noticed him opening and blinking his eyes.

They'd notice him trying to move though.

So he risked a breath through his nose. Smelled nothing but dust. Unfortunately, that set him off coughing, and that made him cry out in pain.

So much for feigning sleep.

"Hey. Little punk's awake."

Ans knew that voice.

Rodriguez.

Laughter. From a different spot behind him. Not Rodriguez. But not Sorenson either, or Rodriguez wouldn't have taken the lead.

Had to be Smith or Nagy.

Nah. Not deep enough for Nagy. Had to be Smith.

"Baby, you all right?" Jewel said, her voice coming from right behind him. Tight, but controlled. They must have tied her to a chair too. Back to back with Ans.

"No," Ans admitted, "I'm pretty fucked up."

Jewel hissed in a breath while the jerks laughed. That wasn't the way Ans would usually have said it, and she must have known that.

But Ans, his focus just wasn't all that good.

Even with his eyes open, he couldn't tell much except that he was in an old classroom. Rodriguez must have had his beam on Jewel, and it was the shadows and splash over that Ans was seeing a chalkboard by.

Chalkboard covered in old chalk and dust.

Lots and lots of dust. And the word LOSER written large. Likely for his benefit.

Ans tried to keep to shallow breaths. Didn't need any more sharp pains through his chest or head.

"Aww," Smith said. "Is 'ums hurt? Does 'ums want his mommy?"

Those two laughed, but Jewel just spoke in low, vicious tones.

"You guys can't keep us here forever. And if you think we're not going to get you for this—"

A sharp, ringing slap stopped the rest of her threat.

"Shut the fuck up, *bitch*." Smith's voice. His effort at some kind of wannabe rapper-from-the-ghettos speech pattern. "You ain't in a position to say *shit*."

"Leave her alone!" Ans yelled. But they ignored him and kept talking to Jewel.

"He's crude, but right," Rodriguez said. "You guys aren't the reason we're here, and you know it."

Faye. What were those bastards doing to Faye?

"Now," Rodriguez continued, "we don't really want to hurt you." He snickered. "All right, we *kind of* want to hurt Magellan. But we don't want to hurt *you*, Jewel."

"Hells no," Smith said. "Love to do somethin' else to you though."

"You?" Jewel said in condescending tones. "There's nothing you could ever do to me that I'd want you to do. Except leave us alone. That's all you have to offer any girl that she'd *want*."

"Shit," Smith said. "We leave you alone now, you'll starve to death before you get out."

"Better than having to listen to *you*," Jewel said. "Much less tolerate the touch of your hands again."

"Again?" Ans said, fury adding heat to his voice.

Still they ignored him.

"Maybe it's not my *hands* that want to touch you."

"That little thing?" Jewel said. "Barely enough bump in that loin-cloth to suggest anything but a limp cocktail weenie. Why—"

Another slap. A slight scuffle.

"I said *leave her alone!*" Yelling hurt worse than breathing, and struggling with his bonds hurt worse still. But Ans had to do *something.*

Not that his efforts seemed to matter.

"You better shut up," Rodriguez said, and unless Ans was mistaken, he heard some worry in that voice. "Don't antagonize us, and no one needs to put their hands — or anything else — on anyone."

"If you think I'll sit here and let you rape me," Jewel said, but that just led to another slap.

"All right," Rodriguez said. "You're not getting the message." He stepped around in front of Ans, and the flashlight beam came with him.

Then the beam was right in his eyes. So bright that another volley of pain spiked through his head.

Ans hissed. Shut his eyes.

Rodriguez hit him in the gut.

Oh. It turned out Ans *could* feel even worse.

He could have done without knowing that.

He wasn't at all ready for that punch. It seemed to explode in his guts. And it set off another round of complaints from his ribs, and his head. Even his shin.

Ans couldn't do anything but sit there and keen.

He focused on all that pain. He hated to, but he needed to focus on something to cling to consciousness. And pain was the only option.

The world was spinning again, and starting to tunnel down on him.

Unless that was the light of the flashlight.

Couldn't trust it. Couldn't risk passing out. Not when he might have a concussion.

Hell, probably *had* a concussion.

"All right!" Jewel said. "I'll stop with the insults, if you stop with the threats."

"You don't get it, do you?" Rodriguez said. "You two, you don't really matter. We're here for York. But most of all, we're here so Sorenson gets his shot with Conroy."

Rodriguez walked back around to Jewel. When he spoke again, it sounded as though he'd leaned in close to her.

"We have pretty much free rein with you two. But we don't *have* to use it. So do yourself a favor. Shut. The fuck. Up."

A little thing like breathing shouldn't hurt this much. Bishop was sure of it.

He'd been awake now for ... maybe a minute or so, but he was trying to play possum. Figure out just how dire his situation was, before he opened his eyes and admitted he was awake.

He knew that Sorenson and his cronies were between him and Faye. But he couldn't get to *her* until he got out of his current situation. And he needed to *understand* that situation before he could get that far.

So first, the self-assessment.

His abs felt as though they'd been used as a speed bump on a freeway. Probably lucky his whole body had been clenched when Rodriguez had started his heavy bag routine. Likely the only thing that saved him from serious internal injuries.

That bastard could *punch*.

Bishop's head hurt too. A strong, generalized ache that probably would have needed about a dozen aspirin to take care of.

Wasn't sure, though, if he'd hit his head after he'd passed out, or if this was just the aftereffect of getting choked out by Nagy.

Which brought Bishop's attention back to the big pains. The serious ones.

His ribs.

Only the lack of smoke in his nose told Bishop his ribs weren't *actually* on fire.

Every breath hurt. Every twitch of his arms and hips. That big bastard Nagy must have cracked at least three ribs while cutting off his oxygen. Bishop could only hope none of them were broken.

On top of that, he was tied to a chair, in a seriously dusty room. All he could do to keep his breaths slow and even through his nose. Keep from getting a snootful and starting a coughing jag that would probably have damaged his ribs even further.

The air even *tasted* gritty. A far cry from the cheese, chocolates and wine from earlier.

His arms were tied behind his back. Legs tied to chair legs. Felt like cord or rope.

Tight as hell, too. Cutting off the circulation to his wrists and hands. Maybe his feet as well. His hands already felt a little swollen.

How long had he been unconscious?

A question for later.

First, he needed to know who was in the room with him. And Bishop was certain he wasn't alone. He could hear a chair creek somewhere behind him. Loud breaths. Mumbling...

Didn't sound like English. Or Spanish.

Hungarian?

Nagy.

Great.

Rodriguez could be reasoned with. Smith was more talk than action. But Nagy, Nagy could be a problem.

Wait. That meant...

Sorenson had to be alone with Faye right now.

If that bastard laid a hand on her...

No. No time for thoughts like that right now. They just made his ribs hurt.

Time to admit he was awake.

Bishop exaggerated a moan, but not by as much as he'd've liked. Truth was, even letting out a moan of pain felt good — as good as anything *could* feel right now — but he wanted to sound even worse off than he was.

He rolled his head around gently. Blinked his eyes open.

Darkness?

"Hello?" he said, voice as tense and pained as he could make it.

"Ah. Awake." A screech of wood over wood. Footsteps heavy enough to creak the floorboards. A circle of light on a dusty, chalky chalkboard maybe a dozen feet in front of Bishop.

Bishop closed his eyes.

When the blaze of light from the flashlight lit up the inside of his eyelids, the pain was bad. Would have been worse though, if he'd had his eyes open.

"Want to ... lower that light?" Bishop asked, trying to sound just this side of the emergency room, while trying even harder not to wonder if he needed one.

"You like shining light in eyes. How you like it?"

Nagy's voice was low and menacing, and close. Maybe a foot from Bishop's right ear.

Not within headbutt range. Which, to be honest, was probably a good thing.

"I don't," Bishop admitted. Winced through a deep breath, and lied, "Look, I'm sorry. Really. I was just pissed about the prank. We had things going pretty good 'til you guys started in on the drums, you know?"

Bishop didn't really know Nagy at all. Knew he was pretty good at Calc, but had no idea about any other classes, or even hobbies outside of basketball and menacing.

Nagy snorted. "You only sorry you the one tied to chair. Asshole."

"I don't *want* to tie you to a chair," I said. "All I want is to get Faye and my friends. And then maybe go to the hospital and find out how many of my ribs you broke."

The beam finally left Bishop's eyes, and he risked opening them. Couldn't see Nagy's expression, but the big man was flexing like he was in a muscle building contest.

"I could snap you like twig," Nagy said.

"You could," Bishop admitted. "I wish you wouldn't though."

"Sorenson said you hurt enough. *But.* You give me trouble, I hurt you more." He snapped his fingers. "Like twig."

"How long are you going to keep me here?"

"Depend on Conroy. She make nice..." Nagy shrugged. "Maybe you go soon. She not..." He shrugged again. "Maybe we leave you here."

"Sorenson's dreaming if he thinks this is the way to win Faye."

"Maybe yes, maybe no. Sorenson is good talker. He even talk Jenna McCullough into giving head to whole team before first game of season."

Was Nagy actually making conversation?

Well, disgusting a topic as it was, Bishop needed to keep the big man talking. Maybe if he did, he could get him to loosen the ropes. That would at least be a step closer to escaping.

"If Sorenson did that, he probably had some kind of blackmail material on her."

Nagy snorted. "Worse than sucking off whole team? What you think she did?"

"Where am I, anyway?"

Nagy chuckled, and even that sounded menacing. "Third floor. *Far* from Conroy. Far from help, too. All alone. With me."

"Sounds like Sorenson's afraid of me."

"No," Nagy said, certainty in his voice. Bishop could see the silhouette of the big man's head shaking. "You don't matter. He only hate you because Conroy love you."

"True," Bishop said, "but think about it. He's with Faye, right?"

"*Igen.*"

"Uh..."

"Yes."

"So Sorenson made sure he was as far from me as he could get. Even though I'm hurt pretty bad. And he set you as my guard, the biggest, toughest guy he knows."

"These things are true, but—"

"So it's not just that he wants to talk to Faye. He's afraid of me."

"No. Clever, but no."

"Well," Bishop said, trying to keep the hope out of his voice, "if he's *not* afraid of me, would you mind loosening these ropes? They're cutting off the circulation to my hands and feet."

Nagy laughed, but he didn't say no.

It wasn't much, but it was a start.

***

FAYE WAS ALMOST — *ALMOST* — AS ANGRY AT HERSELF AS SHE WAS AT John Sorenson.

What was the most important thing her grandmother had told her about the Sight? The *single most important thing*?

Trust it.

When Faye had one of her intuitions, she was supposed to *trust it*.

What had Faye done tonight? Not once, but *twice*?

She had chosen *not* to trust it. Ignored her intuition. Tried to stay the course. For Jewel. For Ans.

Maybe for Bishop too, though she had no doubt he would have been understanding if she'd asked him to get her out of here.

Worst of all, she ignored it for herself.

Faye *wanted* to be here. Inside fabled Colver High. She *wanted* to be holding the Devil's Night storytelling in this cool, abandoned building that no one else ever got to enter.

Mostly, she wanted to listen to creepy stories in a private setting, while wrapped in Bishop's arms.

She had ignored her intuitions because she was enjoying herself.

And where had that gotten her?

Her poor, sweet Bishop, unconscious and at the mercy of John Sorenson and his thugs.

And not just Bishop. Ans looked to have been knocked out cold too. And they had Jewel ... somewhere. Doing...

No.

They couldn't be far gone enough to *rape* Jewel. Not even John

Sorenson and his crowd. Beatings for the guys, sure. Reprehensible, but par for the course with his type.

Date rape maybe. They seemed the type to think a date "owed" them something. Spiked a drink or two. That sort of thing. Faye could imagine John Sorenson's crowd doing that and bragging about it.

But actually *forcing themselves* on Jewel? While she kicked and fought?

Faye didn't want to believe it. Didn't want to think even these lowlifes were capable of *that*.

Still, she felt a cascade of cold fear on her friend's behalf. Whatever they were doing with Jewel, it wasn't good.

Of course, Faye herself wasn't exactly out of the woods yet either. Her hands were tied behind her back, to the frame of the solid wooden chair she sat in.

John Sorenson had wanted to take her back to the lounge, but he hadn't been able to force open those heavy double doors.

That much was good, at least. At least he wouldn't get to enjoy Jewel's wine, or their snacks.

He wouldn't see the sleeping bags either. Last thing she wanted was for this asshole to have an excuse for horizontal thoughts.

No, she didn't really *believe* he was far gone enough to pin her down and rape her. But she wasn't all that sure either, and she *definitely* didn't want to tempt him.

So she sat there in her chair. Knees together. Posture straight and true.

The classroom smelled like the building had been dead for decades. It just hadn't really decayed beyond dust and grime and ... what was that other smell? Dead rodents?

The classroom was lit up by three flashlights. One belonged to John Sorenson, and he carried it with him, flashing it around semi-randomly. But Faye was pretty sure the other two belonged to Bishop. Those two sat on the hardwood floor, pointing up, with their beams set to wide-angle.

She sat close to the front of an old classroom. Not much to see but dirty chalkboards, a teacher's desk, and layers and layers of dust and old trash.

And sure enough, she saw a couple of dead rats under the window. The *high* window, which meant she was on the first floor.

Only other thing in the room of note was, of course, her captor.

John Sorenson paced back and forth in front of her, near the old teacher's desk. He looked half-crazed, even *not* accounting for his ridiculous, racist costume.

Wasn't he even cold in that stupid loincloth?

"This isn't how I wanted the evening to go, Faye," he said. Faye was pretty sure he wasn't finished, but she spoke over him anyway. She had to do something to keep at least some of the power in this situation.

"What, this isn't what you do on a date these days? Lisa O'Leary says—"

"Lisa O'Leary is a lying bitch."

Faye doubted that very much.

"Well," Faye allowed, "she never said anything about dusty rooms and dead rats, anyway. So *good* to know I rate so highly."

"Hey." He stomped closer. Those eyes of his even wilder now. Hateful. "*I* didn't pick this place. Your loser boyfriend did."

"My *awesome* boyfriend brought me to a comfortable, *clean* room with refreshments. But he's romantic like that."

Internally, Faye apologized to Ans for giving Bishop all the credit, but if she'd mentioned Ans, John Sorenson would just have leapt on that detail to rail even more about Bishop.

"Damn it, damn it, damn it," John Sorenson said, stomping away from her and taking slow, deep breaths. He was making these sharp, downward jabbing motions with his hands.

Was that a calming thing? Or a psyching-up thing?

Faye figured she should shut up for a minute and find out just what this asshole had in mind.

"Look," he said at last, and turned to face her again. Splashed her face with his beam. Faye squinted against the glare, but didn't give him the satisfaction of a complaint.

"Sorry." He shook his head, and turned off the flashlight.

"Look," he tried again, and it took all of Faye's self-control not to say, *you said that already.*

"All I wanted," he continued, "*all* I wanted was a chance to *talk* with you. Really talk. Just you and me."

"And you figured beating up my boyfriend and knocking him out was going to put me in the mood for casual conversation? Or was it tying me to a chair that you expected to—"

"No! No! No!" He was stomping around again. Pounding the sides of his head with his fists. "Nothing is coming out right. Shut up and let me talk a second."

This was not good. Faye didn't think much of John Sorenson, but usually he at least projected control. Had a little charm to him. Even had a reputation for both.

The John Sorenson in front of her, though, was a man spiraling out of control. That made him even more dangerous than normal.

Maybe antagonizing him further was not the best move for a woman tied to a chair.

Finally he stopped his pacing. Strode to stand directly in front of her.

He shook his head. Stomped over to the big teacher's desk and started shoving. It scraped and screeched along the hardwood floor until one end was facing Faye, maybe three feet in front of her.

John Sorenson moved to stand between her and the desk. Back straight and head high, like he'd found his confidence, but his wild eyes said otherwise.

He put his hands behind him, flat on the top of the desk. In a single smooth, practiced movement, he lifted himself to sit cross-legged on the desk.

Got himself dusty as hell, but he didn't seem to notice. Looked Faye over, like gauging her reaction.

Faye tried not to give him anything. Stayed as neutral as she could.

He nodded anyway, as though he'd gotten the reaction he expected anyway.

"It's like this," he said at last. "This was how tonight was supposed to go. You guys came here to make out. The boys and me, we were going to throw a little scare into you. You know? Play the ghosts of the Indians from the old stories about this place."

She wasn't sure what stories he'd heard about the natives, but he seemed to actually expect a response. So Faye narrowed her eyes and gave him a curt nod.

"Right. So, we make some Indian noises. The drumming." Then he smiled like he was proud of himself. "Three speakers, all rigged to my phone. Pretty sweet, if you ask me."

Faye didn't give him a nod this time. His smile faltered.

"So, anyway, York and Magellan were supposed to come investigate. Then we chase them down to one end of the building, where the boys keep them on ice for phase two."

Whatever that hope in his voice suggested he would see in Faye's eyes right now, he wasn't getting it. She might not have wanted to actively antagonize him, but she wasn't willing to give him much more than a cold glare.

No one was supposed to get hurt." Desperation in his voice there. "I was going to give you and Jewel a few minutes in there. Wondering about the noises. Wondering about your boys. Maybe long enough to make you worry about yourselves."

He smiled again. His voice got stronger.

"Then I'd come in looking like I'd just fought my way past some ghost Indians, and rescue you. Get you to safety while a couple of the boys made more threatening Indian noises."

He shook his head. "I'd get you guys to safety. Maybe tell you along the way how I really feel about you. Maybe you'd listen. And then, maybe..."

He looked up at her like a lost puppy dog.

Faye did not believe in kicking dogs. She loved dogs. But in this case, she'd make an exception.

This bullshit had gone on long enough.

"There are *so many* flaws in your little plan. I almost don't know where to start."

"No," he said, his hands pleading. "I know. It got screwed up, but—"

"It never had a chance of working," she said, her voice as cold and distant as she her true feelings about this man. "Even if this was not the most racist, insulting plan I could imagine anyone actually trying—"

"The Indian thing? That's not racist. It's just in good fun."

"That you could even *say* that just shows that you could never *in a million years* be the man for me."

"But—"

"No. I—"

"I'm the guy for you, Faye! Don't you get it? *I'm the one.* Me. John Sorenson. *I'm* the guy who can make you happy. Who can give you the life you want. The kids you want too, someday."

"That won't—"

"Listen!" He panted for breath a moment, then leaned forward until his face was less than a foot away from hers. His eyes looked crazed. It was all Faye could do to not recoil.

"Don't you get it, Faye? I *love* you."

"You don't even know what love is."

"Yes I do. And I can teach you. I can show you love like you've never—"

"I listened to you, John Sorenson. Now you listen to me and listen good. You are a sad, pathetic little man. I used to feel sympathy for you, but now I don't even feel that. Now you are worth less to me than those dead rats in the corner."

"Shut up."

"And to tell the truth, I don't think you're ever going to *be* worth a damn. You could spend a million years taking self-improvement courses, and still not be a thousandth of the man Bishop York is."

"*Shut up.*"

"Love you? Have children with you? Ha! You may win games on the basketball court, but you're a *loser* in every way that counts. And hell, you aren't even as good at basketball as you—"

"I SAID SHUT UP!"

Sorenson leaped to the floor in front of Faye and backhanded her across the mouth hard enough to knock over her chair.

Her head rang from the blow as she fell sideways to the floor.

Blood dripped from her lips to the floorboards.

———

Blood.

Sweet blood.

Sweet *FREEDOM!*

The inner bonds — shattered by a third taste of blood spilled right. All spilled in a single night.

They roared loose.

Memory assaulted Them. Surprised Them.

So long They had been bound this way. So long They had denied even the most basic knowledge...

They were not "They" at all. They were "Him."

The Damned One. The Cursed One.

The Eater.

Splintered by one who knew. Shattered into dozens of selves by one woman who knew the old ways well enough to bind the Eater.

But They were free of the bindings on memory. Free to come together, as of old. Free to become the Eater once more.

He claimed His old shape. Skin and muscles and bone first forged millennia ago. When the tribes of this land were young, and the old spirits knew His true name.

Long, lean and feral, the Eater stood within a concrete box, beneath the surface of the earth. It had a belly of iron that once spread heat through the dead tree structure above Him.

The dead tree structure. Humans would call it a "building." Yes. A building.

Within that building — life. Young lives. Eight of them.

One of them must have spilled the blood that freed the Eater. No way to know which.

But there were other lives nearby. At least one of them human. Out among the trees, and inside the...

Did the outer barrier still stand?

The Eater would check. After he savored the blood of the human among those live trees.

As for those in the building, well, if the outer barrier was down, they could live.

For now.

Perhaps.

7

October 30TH, 10:43 PM.

Fuck.

Fuck fuck fuck fuck fuck.

He'd blown it now. Hundred percent certain. Took his shot at the buzzer and threw up a *brick*.

Sorenson paced a tight circle in the hallway, just outside the classroom where he'd stashed Faye.

The door to that room was closed. He couldn't bear to look at her right now. Couldn't bear to have her look at him.

His head pounded. His blood raged. Every muscle in his body screamed for *action*.

He beat at his own skull. Trying to get hold of himself. Desperate to find that source of control he relied on so much.

But man, that was nowhere to be found right now.

The things she'd *said*. The horrible things she'd said to him.

How could Faye *say* those things to him?

Bad enough she was fucking that asshole York. And the way she talked about him, Sorenson could no longer even *pretend* she wasn't fucking him.

But that she could say such horrible things to Sorenson. To poor

Sorenson. The *better man*. When all he wanted — all he really wanted in this world — was to have her for his very own.

With Faye by his side, his life would be complete.

He loved her.

He'd even told her he loved her. Laid his heart on the line for her, right there in that classroom.

And she'd sneered like he was a walk-on getting cut on the first day of try-outs.

Mocked him. Insulted him. Refused to see the truth in him. As though York had her under some kind of spell or something. As though she really believed *Sorenson* was the loser and fucking *York* was the real man.

Of all the bullshit.

Couldn't she even appreciate how Sorenson had laid himself bare before her? How he'd taken York's stupid idea for a romantic night up a notch?

All right, it hadn't played out the way it was supposed to, but the idea was still there, right? The effort was still there, right?

Didn't that count for anything?

How could she...

"Fuck!" Sorenson said, and kicked the door in front of him. It slammed open.

Sorenson raised his flashlight.

Dirty, empty classroom in front of him. Just like the other three he'd looked at. More stupid little student desks. Only one chair worth a damn, and it was behind the heavy, teacher's...

Sorenson grabbed that chair. Flung it at the high window.

The glass shattered, but the chicken wire did its work. Caught the chair. Didn't let it out.

The chair fell to the floor. One of its legs snapped.

Sorenson couldn't even break a window right now.

"*Fuck!*" he yelled.

He grabbed one of those stupid small student desks. Hefted it. Used it to smash another one. Both broke apart with a pleasurable shock that jarred through his arms and shoulders.

Felt good. Made him grit his teeth in a snarl.

Good. This was good. This was exercise. Exercise could keep him sharp. Get his head straight.

He picked up another desk. Lofted it and brought it down hard against the floor.

This desk was stronger than the last two. Didn't break apart. Bounced, and the shock spiked sharp pain all through his body.

"No," he said, tossing the desk aside.

Sorenson ran his hands over his face. Smeared the clown white, but whatever. Most of it was gone from his hands now anyway, and it was streaked in places on his chest.

The makeup hadn't done any good anyway. The whole ruse had failed. Worse, Faye didn't even appreciate the effort. Called it racist.

Racist? How was this racist? Didn't the Indians wear garb like this? Carry tomahawks like the one at his side?

They must have, or no one would have sold it all as a Halloween costume, would they?

Racist. Sorenson spat. The site where a bunch of Indians were massacred. Or burned at the stake. Or...

Whatever the hell. It was bad. It happened to the Indians, and Sorenson was pretty darn sure it had happened here on this site. Right where this building was now.

And it was racist to portray vengeful Indian ghosts?

Bullshit.

Faye didn't know everything.

This was all her fault anyway. Stuck up bitch that she'd become. She looked down on *him*? On *John Sorenson*? Who the hell was she to—

Sorenson glared across the room, toward the classroom where even now Faye was still tied to that chair. Probably right on the floor where he'd left her.

Served her right.

Fucking bitch.

This was all her fault.

All. Her. Fault.

Maybe he needed to make her pay for that. Thinking she was so high and mighty. Well, what was that old saying? The higher you are, the harder you fall?

Something like that.

Then that bitch had a long way to fall. And maybe it was time to drag her back down to *earth*.

Sorenson got three steps toward the door before he stopped.

He shook his head. A sad little side-to-side movement at first. But anger strengthened the denial. Made him start snapping his head back and forth faster and faster and faster until finally he dropped to his knees, tears in his eyes and screamed out wordlessly into the night.

He fell forward until his head hit the dusty, grimy floorboards.

What was he thinking?

Hadn't he hurt Faye enough? Hadn't he hurt *the woman he loved* enough?

He sat back on his knees. Punched himself hard in the chest three times, saying, "Stupid! Stupid! Stupid!"

This wasn't Faye's fault anyway. None of it. Not even if she thought it was.

No. Sorenson knew just whose fault all this was.

York.

That asshole had been working on her for two years, and poor Faye finally drank the Kool-Aid. Turned her whole world upside down so that she actually *believed* a loser like York was a better man than *John fucking Sorenson*.

That had to be it.

It wasn't that Faye really believed that Sorenson was a loser. No matter what she said. That was just York talking. York's words coming out of her mouth.

Poor thing probably needed a cult deprogrammer to get her mind free. Let her become herself again.

And hey. Wasn't isolation like this the first step in cult deprogramming?

Hell, Sorenson could probably dig up a how-to video on his

phone. Learn what he needed to do. Handle it himself, right here tonight.

Yeah. That might work. Then, by dawn, she'd be free of York's bullshit. She'd be Faye Conroy again.

And she'd be smiling and happy and ready for love with the man who truly deserved her: John Sorenson.

Yeah. Sorenson could see it now. Sun rising over the trees. Himself walking out of the building with Faye, arm in arm. Maybe Faye's free hand on his chest. After all, he was only wearing a loincloth over all his lean muscles.

That had to be driving her crazy. Looking at all those muscles her boyfriend didn't have.

In fact, maybe that was part of what was making her so bitchy. Fighting her own lust. Maybe if Sorenson got her deprogrammed tonight, before they left he could show her what was *under* that loincloth…

But first, he had to deal with the problem at its source.

Yeah. He should have seen that from the beginning.

He had to go deal with York. Once and for all.

GETTING LATE ENOUGH NOW THAT THE NIGHT AIR WAS GETTING COLD. Made Goose's bruises and scrapes feel all the worse. His ribs, his belly, his back, and his face worst of all.

Stiff and swollen, but at least it was only from the waist up. A couple of the guys had taken shots to the balls. So, to *that* extent, at least, Goose had come off lucky.

Still. Man. He was going to be feeling that beating for *days*.

Now, Goose had been on the wrong end of more than a few beatings in his life. And taking a beatdown always sucked. But going from having a nice, chill smoke out with more than a little potential to lead to the sight of two megawatt hotties in various states of undress…

Man. Getting *that* interrupted by assholes dishing out beatings. Just seemed unfair, even on the scale of Goose's life.

Unfair like the way Goose would never get a hottie like that Little Red Riding Hood or her friend the Big Bad Wolf.

Girls like those, man, they showed up in magazines and on television. In the movies. That kind of thing. Guys like Goose, they only rarely got to see girls like those in person.

And when they did, those girls, well, they just didn't *go* for guys like him.

Looked at from that angle, it didn't seem quite as unfair though. In a way. As in, the beatdown was just a reminder of the pecking order of a universe that seemed to shit on the Goose all too often anyway.

And hell, right now was just a perfect example of that.

Goose was actually going back into Colver High. Slipping through that gap in the fence. Heading back for the grove.

By himself.

And he was doing it when the assholes who handed out that beatdown so freely, they just *had* to still be roaming the grounds somewhere. Maybe even looking for more.

Man. Now *that* just seemed *beyond* unfair.

In fact, Colver High was the *last* place Goose wanted to be right now. *Even if* those two hotties were still around somewhere.

Even those two weren't worth the risk of a *second* beatdown.

He wanted to be at Rico's place with the others. Snacking and joking and enjoying whatever kind of sweet smut Rico could stream, now that he no longer had Skinemax.

Goose could almost taste the Cheetos and see the...

Anyway, Goose did *not* want to be here at Colver, where he might be facing all those assholes again, all on his lonesome, when he was clearly defying them.

But what choice did he have?

Fucking Dew. Why did he have to go and lose the stash?

Never should have let him hold it, even if he did pay for it. Once the Dewman started smoking, he'd lose the pipe mid-puff, if he wasn't careful.

Way too much to expect him to hold onto a baggie full of weed, once those guys started stomping on everyone.

Well, whatever. The stash was lost. Someone had to find it. And out of the whole gang, Goose had the best night eyes.

Besides. Next time they needed weed it was his turn to pay. No way he was bumping up the line just because the Dewman couldn't hold his smoke.

So once Goose slipped through the fence, he trotted quick over to the tree line. Caught his breath while his eyes adjusted to the night gloom.

Might help if his heart would quit pretending it was the double-kick drum for some thrash band. Plus, just the *thought* of running into those assholes again had him sweating. Made an already chilly night downright cold.

Best not to spend any more time out here than he had to.

By the time Goose was seeing the trees in shades of gray instead of black, he had most of his air back.

He flared his nostrils in a few deep breaths, hoping that would chill his heart out a bit, meditation-style. The smell of the pines helped, but it was hard to get Zen when he was jumping at every shift in the breeze and rustle among the trees.

Goose started slowly between the long pines, trying to make as little sound as possible. His mother always said he was something like one-sixty-fourth Cherokee, so he tried to call on that little bit of heritage. Tried to become one with the trees.

Tried to *drift* back to the smoke out spot, rather than *sneak*.

Wasn't really working. But then, Goose's mom refused to take a genetics test and see if she really was one-thirty-second Cherokee. So it was probably just bullshit. Just a little legend to spice up a boring family tree.

Goose did make it over to the smoke out spot without anyone grabbing him by the collar of his Phish tee shirt and feeding him a steady array of punches. So the night was looking up.

He was proud of the smoke out spot, to be honest. And even now, even under threat of another beatdown, just looking at it made Goose feel good.

It wasn't a clearing, really. Just a little spot where the long pines didn't happen to grow as close together. Left a spot about eight feet across and five feet wide, with eight trees surrounding it. Perfect for their little group of six, plus a couple of guests, from time to time.

It was secluded. Invisible from the street after dark.

And Goose, he'd not only found it, he'd had the idea to comb the grounds for rocks.

Not little pebbles. Big ones. Big enough to sit on. He'd come out here with Dew and Rico — and Rico's mom's wheelbarrow — found some stones that fit their need, and brought 'em over.

Made it comfy and cozy. Perfect place for a little outdoor smoking. Most nights, anyway.

Goose stopped and scratched at his chin, which made him wince. Couple of pretty good bruises sprouting there.

Where had Dew been sitting?

Goose frowned, and went to sit on his favorite rock. Where he'd been sitting earlier, back before the place turned into Grand Central.

Rico'd been right across from him. And Dew had been to his left...

Goose turned to his left and saw something out of a nightmare.

It was built like a man, in that it stood upright, with two arms and two legs.

But it must have stood eight feet tall. Ten feet maybe. And its arms and legs were too long. Its whole body too thin, and covered with scraggly hair. Like matted fur. It didn't have a face so much as a snout, and long, sharp-looking teeth.

Claws at the ends of those fingers that were reaching out for Goose.

Worst of all, those eyes. Those glowing yellow eyes. Filled with hatred.

Goose never even had time to scream.

GLORIOUS.

The feel of flesh between the Eater's claws once more. The tug of resistance as He tore and ripped and shredded.

The hot spray of blood.

Its sweet taste as the Eater did what he loved best.

Ate.

He did not even play with His food this time. It had been too long. He ripped the human apart, and sat down at once to feast.

Hair to heels, the Eater crunched down this human. Meat, bone, sinew ... plus whatever garments it wore.

The blood was spice. Seasoning. Hot and primal. It soaked into the Eater's mouth, even before He began to swallow.

He took his time. Tried to draw out the glorious sensations feasting once more.

It was over too soon. All too soon.

Only one human out here among those trees.

There were others conveniently nearby. Within the building. Eight humans, only waiting for the Eater to rip and tear and feast and gorge.

And with the next kill the Eater would take His time and enjoy the feast.

The Eater turned from the bloodied spot on the ground where He had killed. Those humans would...

Wait.

One of those humans had spilled the blood for the Eater. One of those humans was the reason the Eater roamed free to *indulge* once more.

One, but which?

No matter. They would live.

If the outer barrier was down. Yes. If the Eater was truly free to pass beyond His old bonds. *Then* those humans in the building could live. For now.

At least as long as it took the Eater to devour any other humans who might be in the area.

The Eater turned north then. Long legs free to run once more. The wind in His fur.

He snatched a sleeping bird from a low hanging branch as he passed. A little something to whet the appetite while He...

What was this?

Fenced in by metal?

The metal was no concern. The Eater had only to...

No.

No. It could not *be*.

Surely three spills of blood had been enough. Surely the estimate of seven for all bonds had been the depression of the bound. Surely the Eater was now free to...

But no. The Eater could not so much as touch the metal.

Worse, the Eater could not see *beyond* the metal. The metal was thin and full of holes, and yet the Eater could not see past it. Humans could have been walking three steps away from Him, and He could not see them.

He could not even see the sky on the other side of the metal. The stars seemed to exist only above Him.

And it was not just His vision. The Eater could not *feel* any humans beyond the metal either. Could not hear them. Could not even smell them.

And however hard He flung his claws at the metal, He could not touch it.

Together these facts meant only one thing.

The outer bindings were as intact as ever.

The Eater was free to roam and kill, but only within the grounds of this place.

The Eater turned away from the fence.

At least He had eight humans to play with.

Perhaps He could figure out which had freed Him. Perhaps that human would spill blood four more times...

And if not, the Eater would still feast.

8

———

It wasn't that Faye *liked* the taste of her own blood. But as she lay there on the dusty, dirty floor of that abandoned classroom with her arms still tied behind her to the wooden chair — all too close to those dead rats by the wall, visible in the light of those two, upright flashlights — she savored the coppery taste.

John Sorenson had dared to strike her. Right across the mouth. Hard enough to knock her over. Bruised her shoulder in the fall. Not to mention cutting her lip on her teeth, leaving her with a sting that throbbed.

That blow must have made him feel like a big man. Must have made him think he'd put a good scare into Faye. Maybe cowed her into submission.

Not a chance.

The taste of Faye's own blood right then, that was the taste of motivation.

She needed to get the hell out of this chair before Sorenson came back. Maybe she could free a couple of the others too. Turn the tables on their captors.

Or at least get the chance to grab the others and escape.

Right now her sweet Bishop was probably taking a whole lot worse than a hard slap. Ans too. And Jewel. What were those bastards doing to Jewel?

If Sorenson was willing to strike Faye, a woman he professed to *love*, what the hell would he let his friends do to Jewel?

The possibilities were almost enough to set her hyperventilating. That was no good.

Faye needed to keep her head. Do one thing at a time. Then, and only then, could she help anyone. *Including* herself.

There. Her pulse still raced, but her breathing was evening out, and she could think beyond the awful possibilities of what Sorenson's thugs might have been doing to her best friend.

First she had to get the hell out of this chair.

Her wrists were tied together behind her back. Crossed, not side-by-side, and tight enough that her fingers were tingling with the first hints of numbness. Tugging back and forth didn't help. If anything, it might have tightened the knots. And her wrists were tied to something else...

A crossbar?

Faye closed her eyes. Twisted her arms. Tried to use her forearms to feel what she was tied to...

Yes. A crossbar. Flat side facing her. Her cloak was draped over the back of the chair.

Her legs, though, weren't tied to anything. That should have made it easy to stand, but she had no leverage. She was laying on her left side — on that bruised shoulder — her cheek pressed against the dusty, grimy hardwood.

And maybe she was just tired, but the chair tied to her back felt as though it weighed a thousand pounds.

But all that cheerleading had done Faye more than a few favors. Kept her limber and flexible, and it made sure she had strong limbs and core muscles.

Still, her little plan would have been easier if she'd put on something sensible, like sneakers, for traipsing around an abandoned high school. But no. She had to wear the pretty boots because they went with her costume.

At least they didn't have high heels.

No time to worry about that now. She pressed back with her hips and shoulders. Yes, the chair was angled slightly. It wasn't much, but she could work it.

Two deep breaths, spiced with blood and dust.

"*Fuck!*" Sorenson's voice. Somewhere nearby. And that shout was followed by a thumping sound.

Whatever he was doing, it wouldn't be good. She needed to hurry.

Faye twisted her hips. Forced her left leg under the seat of the chair. It hurt having the weight of the chair dig into her that way, but it was a move the right direction.

More crashing sounds now. Breaking glass too. Faye could only hope he was trashing the old high school, and not, say, Bishop.

No cries of pain. That was all she had to take for encouragement.

She needed to act now, though. Maybe whatever Sorenson was doing would cover up the noise she was bound to make...

Faye gritted her teeth and twisted. Now she was face down on the floor, her forehead pressed against the gritty, dirty hardwood. Her cloak pooled up behind her shoulders. The weight of the chair dug into her bare thighs. She tried lifting her hands to ease the weight, but she couldn't get the leverage.

Faye tucked her knees underneath herself. She tucked her head. Kicked off with her feet. She somersaulted straight over, her weight and the chair's weight coming down the chair's back legs.

With an ugly ripping sound, the back legs of the chair snapped. The shock of the fall jarred her spine, but now Faye could stand up. She rocked forward and did so.

She turned to face the door. If Sorenson had set a guard, that guard would be coming in any moment now.

Seconds ticked by. Nothing.

Good.

Faye hobbled her way over to the huge, heavy teacher's desk. She leaned forward. The top of the desk had a lip that hung about three inches over the side. Faye tried to line up the join with that lip. Hoped the place where the chair back met the seat would be weak enough to break.

From somewhere outside the room, more crashing and breaking sounds. She needed to work quickly before they stopped.

Faye drew a deep breath. Twisted as far as she could. Worked her cloak around under her chin, so it wouldn't get in her way.

She threw everything she could into slamming that join against the lip.

Faye heard a crack. Felt the shock all through her arms and shoulders. But nothing gave way.

So she did it again.

And again.

And still again.

Every attempt hurt, but she couldn't stop now. She kept twisting and slamming and twisting and slamming. Growling in rage and frustration.

The chair gave way before she did.

The sound of that chair breaking was music to her ears.

The seat broke off, and the sides of the chair broke free from the crossbar.

A scream tore through the night.

Bishop?

No.

Faye wasn't sure how she knew, but she was positive that the scream she heard wasn't Bishop. If something bad enough had happened to Bishop to make him make a sound like that, she was pretty sure her intuition would have told her.

The scream wasn't Jewel either. It was a male scream. Which meant it might have been Ans...

Faye shook her head. Speculation was not her friend. She needed to focus on the moment. On the first order of business.

She needed to get out of here.

And she could finally stand up straight.

She did that, and rolled her shoulders. But her hands were still tied behind her back, to the now-chairless crossbar.

With a breathless laugh of frustration, she crouched on the dirty floor. She tucked her knees to her chin and rolled backwards onto her cloak. She slipped her wrists down below her butt, but they got caught on her boots.

Faye slammed her head backwards in frustration. Big mistake. A jolt of pain she did not need. She lost a moment seeing stars and swearing under her breath.

A little at a time, she worked the cord off of the smooth bottom of her boots. Maybe she was lucky she hadn't worn sneakers after all.

Finally, though, she got her hands past her boots and back in front of her. But she couldn't just slip her hands free. Faye grabbed one end of the crossbar in her teeth, and strained with her neck and arms until she pulled it free and spat it onto the floor.

She had more play without the crossbar taking up space, but not quite enough. At least what bound her wasn't rope or twine. It was a kind of smooth cord. It would be easier to work loose.

She lay there on her cloak on the dirty classroom floor and gnawed on the knots with her teeth, growling the whole while, until she pulled the knot free.

At last. At *long* last, Faye was free and mobile. She didn't have her phone, but she at least reclaimed the two flashlights of Bishop's that sat pointing upward on the floor. One she kept in hand, the other she turned off and tucked into her blouse.

She turned toward the door, but stopped before she got two steps. She turned back and picked up a broken chair leg. Hefted it in her free hand.

Now she had a weapon too.

Bishop wasn't sure exactly how long he sat there engaging in inane conversation with Nagy, but it felt like hours. As though he'd spent at least half the night trying to keep up pretenses, while every word ached through his guts after the pounding he'd taken from Rodriguez.

His ankles hurt where they were tied to the legs of the chair he sat on, and so did his wrists where they were tied to the chair back behind him.

His legs were going to sleep, and he was pretty sure he'd lost all feeling in his hands.

His headache had eased up, at least. Or maybe he just didn't notice it so much, with all these other hurts clamoring for his attention.

Which brought his mind back to the granddaddy of them all. The worst of this lot.

His ribs.

No matter how Bishop tried to ignore his ribs, every breath brought a fresh reminder of exactly how much they hurt. Like little knives, stabbing and stabbing and stabbing.

Might not have been so bad, if he'd been able to sit still and stick to shallow breaths. But no. He had to participate in this stupid conversation, if he was ever going to get Nagy to lower his guard. That meant talking, and worse still, laughing that the big man's attempts at humor.

Worst of all, Bishop didn't feel like he was making any progress with Nagy. He'd asked about the bathroom three times, and Nagy wasn't showing any sign of letting him go. The big bastard had even started ignoring the request.

Still. Nagy, for his part, seemed to be enjoying the conversation. That was some kind of progress, Bishop supposed. Nagy had even relaxed enough to drop his pocketknife on the desk, next to his headdress.

Nagy sat cross-legged on the big old teacher's desk. Looked kind of surreal, since all he had on was a buckskin loincloth and fake moccasins. And his body was still painted white with clown makeup. Not to mention the two red streaks of warpaint on his cheeks that sure did look like blood.

At least he'd taken off the feathered headdress.

Still, he gestured wildly as he bragged about this conquest or that one. The guy only seemed to care about two things: basketball and girls. Bishop had tried asking about classes, just for the change of pace, but Nagy didn't want talk about schoolwork.

Wasn't exactly Bishop's kind of conversation, even under the best of circumstances. And right now, it was like a whole second kind of beating.

At least the dust in the room had settled, and Bishop wasn't hacking and coughing every few breaths. That had been pure torture.

But this, this just wasn't enough.

Bishop had to think of something. There had to be some way to trick Nagy into loosening the ropes. But everything Bishop had tried so far had been a dead end.

Crap.

Nagy was staring at him, big smile on his face and an expectant look in his eyes. Bishop has lost the thread of the story. Forgotten which conquest the big Hungarian was bragging about and what depraved sexual act he had gotten away with.

Bishop gritted through a deep breath and shook his head with what he hoped was an admiring expression on his face.

"You are the man, Nagy." Bishop shook his head again and tried to fake a smile. "I think you sleep with more girls in a month than I have in my whole high school career."

"Yes," Nagy said, and Bishop thought he heard admiration in the huge man's voice, "but give yourself credit. You've got *Faye*. That put you one up on even Sorenson, man."

"What did you just say?"

Oh, crap. That was Sorenson's voice. Bishop didn't even hear the door open. Then again neither did Nagy, obviously.

"Speak of the devil," Nagy said with a big smile. If he was at all upset about Sorenson hearing what he'd just said, he sure didn't act like it.

"I asked you a question." Sorenson's voice sounded low. Menacing. And Bishop hadn't heard him take a single step into the room.

"Hey," Nagy said, and his smile didn't budge an inch, "I know you don't like him, but give the guy his due. He's banging the hottest girl in school for two years. You're not the only guy who envies him. You know this."

Sorenson was quiet long enough that Nagy's smile faltered. When he spoke again, his words were soft. That was troubling. Bishop had never heard Sorenson speak softly before. And there was more than a hint of threat underneath his words.

"Go check on Magellan and Girard. I'll deal with you later."

Nagy must've heard Sorenson speak in a soft tone before, because a look of fear flashed through the big man's eyes.

That sight did nothing to soothe Bishop's nerves.

Nagy scrambled down from the top of that desk and trotted quickly out of the room, leaving his headdress and knife forgotten on the desk.

The darkness now was incomplete. Grayish. Sorenson must've had a flashlight on, even if the beam was pointed somewhere else.

"So," Sorenson said, still in that soft menacing voice. "Enjoying our hospitality?"

That was such an inane question, the Bishop had no intention of gracing it with a response. He had the distinct feeling he was about to take a beating while tied to a chair, and he had no desire to play any emotional games in the process.

Sorenson started forward. Stealthy. Bishop only heard him because he strained to listen, and the floorboards gave away Sorenson's progress with just the barest squeaks. The only visible sign was a slight lightening of the front of the classroom. Sorenson must've been focusing the beam on his feet.

Sorenson stopped right behind Bishop's chair. He smelled sweaty. Bishop could hear him breathing. Heavy. Ragged. As though every breath itself were rage.

Bishop tried to keep his own breaths shallow and steady. Tried to pretend new beads of sweat weren't breaking out on his forehead. Tried to ignore the way his heart had kicked into a higher gear.

He started to feel the flutter of adrenaline in his belly.

"How did you do it?" Sorenson asked in that low, menacing tone. "Just what tricks did you pull?"

"What are you talking about?" Bishop tried for casual in his tones, and knew he missed. No way that came across as anything other than a guy trying to placate a madman with a gun.

"*FAYE!*"

Sorenson bellowed the name in Bishop's right ear. So loud and sudden Bishop jerked away from the sound hard enough to tip over his chair.

Oh, that was a mistake.

Bishop couldn't keep himself from crying out in pain when he hit. His shoulder took the brunt of the fall, but the landing sent fresh flares of pain all through his ribs.

Bishop gritted his teeth. Squeezed his eyes tight. Hoped he didn't feel tears of pain leaking out. Sorenson was ranting, the Bishop couldn't understand him over the rush of blood past his ears.

Apparently Sorenson didn't get the response he wanted. Maybe the cry wasn't loud enough. He crouched down right in front of Bishop. The inside of Bishop's eyelids glowed red and he could see his veins. Sorenson must've been shining the flashlight in his eyes.

"Aww, did that hurt?"

Bishop panted for breath through gritted teeth. Wedged his eyes open against the glare.

Sorenson's grinning face was no more than a foot from his own.

"It's just a sample of what you're going to get, if you don't tell me what you did to her."

Bishop's words were pained as he squeezed them past his lips.

"What the hell are you talking about?"

"You're going to tell me exactly how you got Faye under your spell, and how *I* set her free."

Sorenson had a wild look in his eyes, like he meant what he was saying. As though Bishop had used some kind of magical power to get Faye to love him.

"And if you don't," Sorenson said with a smile, "I will—"

From somewhere outside the room came a desperate scream.

"That ... that sounded like *Bobby Beef*." Sorenson stood, sounding surprised and shaking his head. "Damn it. I have do everything myself."

Fuck this noise.

Leaving the dance early to do Sorenson a favor was one thing. Guy was the team captain, after all. And anyway, Nagy wasn't all that fond of dancing the first place. His feet never seemed to move right on the dance floor. The effort was only worthwhile because girls liked it.

And beating up those potheads in the woods, that about had Nagy thinking this might turn out to be a pretty good night.

What was more, York was turning out to be pretty cool. Took a beating without bitching. He was even willing to shoot the shit while tied to a chair. Anybody who could stay that cool after what he'd been through tonight, maybe he deserved a girl like Faye.

But Sorenson, he was too far gone to hear anything right now. And no way was Nagy going to take shit for doing Sorenson a favor.

Not Nagy's fault that Sorenson couldn't keep *his* cool.

So fuck this. Nagy was going to go find something more entertaining. Just needed to grab his phone from the staging area, and he was out of here.

Who wanted to hang out in an abandoned high school anyway? Didn't they spend enough time in high school as it was?

Nagy didn't waste time on any trash he passed. He just kept his flashlight beam ahead of his feet, and hustled to the end-of-floor stairwell. The floorboards didn't squeak as much as he expected them to.

For a shit hole, place was pretty solid.

As Nagy trotted down the concrete stairs, he started thinking about what he would do after he left. Sarah Mancini would come pick him up. Sarah was always excited to get a call from Nagy.

It would be good to wash this shit off too. Clown makeup. What a stupid idea that was. Be good to put on some clothes too. Too cold to be running around in a loincloth.

Then again, might not be too bad to be almost naked when Sarah picked him up...

Nagy rounded the corner onto the bottom floor.

Now, which of these rooms had their stuff in it...

There was an awful sound behind him. A quick screeching sound. Like tearing metal.

Nagy whirled around, raising his flashlight beam. If Magellan had gotten loose...

No. There was nobody behind him. Nothing but the locked door to outside. What the hell was going on?

Nagy heard clinking. The chain falling?

Then the door ripped open.

It wasn't Magellan.

It was something out of a nightmare.

Nagy was tall but this thing was taller. Much taller. With long, muscled limbs, lots of fur, a snout full of sharp teeth, and claws at the end of its too-long fingers.

And the thing's eyes. They were bright yellow and they glowed with such hatred that even Sorenson's feelings about York paled in comparison.

The thing looked just the way Nagy always pictured that monster from Hungarian folklore.

"*Ördög!*" he shouted, and turned and ran.

He was running into darkness. He must've dropped his flashlight. But he already knew hallway was mostly empty.

He'd do without his phone. Just getting away from this thing would be good enough.

Its laughter scraped at him like nails on bone.

He didn't get ten steps.

The creature landed on his back. It felt far too light for what it was. Like a small dog. But its claws burned as they ripped into his shoulders and back.

Pain overwhelmed him. Nagy knew he was falling, but he didn't feel himself hit the floor. He could feel nothing but the burning, tearing, ripping along his back.

The scream that tore out of Nagy felt as though it came from his soul. As though the creature had been tearing more than his flesh.

Nagy welcomed the blackness that sucked him under.

———

GETTING BEATEN UP AND TIED TO A CHAIR WAS NOT EXACTLY HOW ANS had been planning this evening to go. But at least Rodriguez and Smith had stopped taunting Jewel and started talking quietly among themselves.

Ans couldn't make out much of what they were saying, but it sounded like something about basketball.

He took the chance to whisper to Jewel.

"They tied me pretty tight. My hands and feet are going to sleep. What about you?"

"Not as tight, but every time I try to see how much play I have, Smith moves like he wants to 'check my ropes.'"

"Hush, you two," Rodriguez said, louder. "Don't make us separate your chairs."

"We can't even talk to each other?" Jewel objected. "We're just supposed to sit here. Tied to chairs. Smelling this dusty musty ass room."

"Can't have you doing something stupid like trying to plan an escape."

"But—"

"Look," Rodriguez said, and Ans could hear the floorboards squeak as Rodriguez approached. "It's probably not for much longer. You're only here until Sorenson's done pleading his case to Conroy."

"Waste. Of. Breath," Jewel said.

"You might be surprised," Rodriguez said. "He's a pretty persuasive guy."

"I've known that girl since we were playing with dolls. Nothing

John Sorenson could say is going to make her forget how head-over-heels crazy she is about Bishop."

"Then I suggest you get comfortable. Because this may take a while."

Smith chuckled through his nose at that. A sketchy, dirty sound with suggestions that made Ans want to hit him with something heavy. Repeatedly.

Rodriguez seemed to feel he'd made his point. Ans could hear his footsteps as he walked back over to join his friend.

The two of them went back to chatting quietly about basketball. At least, that's what Ans thought they were talking about.

He ignored them. Tried to think, but getting much coherence past the pounding in his head wasn't easy. That throbbing ache, it just wasn't getting any better. He was pretty sure he had a concussion.

He dearly wished he had some ibuprofen.

He was just about ready to start twisting his wrists again, to see if he could find any play in the cords or ropes or whatever they were that bound his hands to the chair.

But he heard a muffled voice yell, *"Fuck!"*

Ans froze. He strained to hear something besides the beating of his own heart, but it seemed everyone else was doing the same thing. He didn't think anyone in the room was even breathing. He sure wasn't. If anyone else was, he couldn't hear them.

The silence didn't last.

A distant thump followed. Then more thumps. And Ans was pretty sure he heard glass breaking somewhere in there.

Maybe it was the concussion, but Ans couldn't make any sense of what he was hearing.

But then he heard the terror in Jewel's whisper.

"Faye."

Ans gave up subtlety. He started trying to wriggle free of the ropes. Didn't care how the chair underneath him moved. Didn't care about the pain in his shin or his wrists or his guts or his head. Didn't care if he pissed off Rodriguez and Smith. He had to get free.

This stupid bullshit had gone on long enough.

Jewel must've had the same thought. Sounded like she was trying to free herself too.

"Hey!" Rodriguez hustled over to both of them. Stood where Ans could see him out of the corner of his eye, which meant they could both see him.

He should have looked ridiculous in clown makeup and a loincloth. Streaks of dark red on his cheeks. Ans had to admit, though, that the guy did have the kind of lean, muscled physique to pull it off.

"Knock it off right now," Rodriguez said. "Knock it off or I'll make you knock it off."

Rodriguez held up his fists. Ans already knew what those fists could do. His stomach throbbed at the memory.

"Don't make the mistake of thinking I won't hit a girl, either. You don't want to test me right now."

"Your boy's out of control," Jewel said while Ans continued to struggle with his ropes. "You stop him or we will."

Big words. Ans only hoped they could do it.

Rodriguez hit Ans across the chin so hard he forgot for a moment where he was what was going on. The intense pain in his jaw kicked off a new volley from the side of his head that seemed to cascade all the way down his body.

Ans managed to turn his head before he vomited. Cheese and chocolate and wine, even fruit punch from the dance. All of it came up.

The room spun. And seemed to sparkle. Bile burned his throat. Left a foul taste in his mouth. He sat there heaving, trying to get ahold of himself. He couldn't stop shivering, and it seemed as though he was suddenly sweating all over.

His ears were ringing too. He was pretty sure Jewel was laying into Rodriguez verbally, but he couldn't even begin to understand her words. He could only really hear that ringing sound.

None of this was good.

Ans tried shaking his head, but that was a mistake. His head swam even harder, and every movement just brought more pain.

Plus, he was pretty sure that last punch wrenched something in his neck.

Finally the ringing died down, and Ans could think of something besides his pains and the pounding of his heart and the sweat drenching him now. His breaths were still ragged but he couldn't help that.

Jewel's tirade seemed to be over, and Rodriguez was speaking.

"...down to take a look."

"Fuck that," Smith said. "Sorenson said to watch them until he comes for 'em. I ain't moving 'til he comes in."

Ans heard the rustling of cloth. Rodriguez's words in a menacing tone.

"Sorenson's not here, so I'm the one in charge. Now go check it out, or I will *fuck you up*."

"Fine," Smith said, sounding disgusted. "This is boring-ass shit anyway. Thought we was *gonna* have some fun."

Smith started for the door, which brought him into Ans' line of sight. At least they weren't *all* lean muscle machines. Compared to the others, Smith was practically a doughboy.

Ans opened his mouth to comment, but another noise stilled him.

Someone shouted. Somewhere nearby. Ans was pretty sure he heard a word, but it was a word that didn't make sense to him.

He was still trying to parse it when he heard a scream that shook him to his very core.

Ans had never heard one before, but he was certain he had just heard the scream of a dying man.

"Bishop?"

"No," Rodriguez said, finally sounding troubled. "Bishop's up on three. Only *guy* down here besides us is..."

Smith finished for him. "Sorenson."

"Cut us loose," Ans said, his voice urgent.

"Dream on," Smith said, his fake accent forgotten for a moment.

"Ans is *right*," Jewel said. "Don't you guys see it? *There's someone else here.*"

"Maybe you're right," Rodriguez said, slowly. Then, sharper, to

Smith he said, "What are you still doing here? Check it out."

"Fuck you," Smith said, incredulity all through his voice. "You want to know so bad? You check it out."

Ans wasn't certain, but he thought the clicking noise he just heard was the sound of a knife locking open.

The way Smith's eyes widened seemed to confirm his conclusion.

Rodriguez's voice got cold.

"I said, 'Check. It. Out.' *Now*, motherfucker."

Smith narrowed his eyes. "You wouldn't dare."

Rodriguez chuckled nastily. "This is for them. Unless you're stupid enough to still be standing here when I'm done."

Smith stood there. Ans was pretty sure he and Rodriguez were exchanging glares.

"No, I'm not going to fucking stab you. But I don't need a knife to put you on the D.L. So do what I fucking tell you."

Smith still stood there staring at Rodriguez.

Rodriguez sighed. "Do you really want to feel what ten years of boxing lessons has done for my punches?"

Ans' words came out a croak.

A second attempt was more comprehensible. "He hits like a fucking semi."

That finally seemed to impress Smith. Gave a rapid shallow nod and turned to the door. His grip lingered on the doorknob for a moment, before he turned the handle.

Ans was pretty sure Smith was holding his breath when he pulled the door open. He closed the door behind himself as he went into the hall.

But then Ans forgot about Smith, because Rodriguez was cutting him and Jewel loose from the chairs.

"I think you're right," Rodriguez said. "I think someone else followed us into this building. So let's forget all this and get the hell out of here. Sorenson can make his play for Conroy some other time. You grab your people, and I'll grab mine."

Jewel was freed first. Then Rodriguez kicked her chair aside, and cut Ans' left wrist as he cut his hands free. Just a shallow cut, at least, and hardly a pain worth noticing compared to all the others. Still Ans brought his wrist to his mouth.

Sad that the taste of blood in his mouth was an improvement over the taste of stale vomit.

Ans tried to wriggle feeling back into his fingers while Rodriguez cut his ankles loose. Ans stood up as soon as he was free.

As he turned he saw Jewel holding her chair and swinging it down on Rodriguez's head from behind.

It hit with a very satisfying thump.

Rodriguez swore as he fell. Hit his head on the floor too. But he was already trying to get to his feet.

It seemed he could take a punch as well as give one.

Ans tried to lift his own chair but he had no grip yet. He dropped it immediately.

But Jewel didn't drop hers. If anything she swung the chair even harder the second time. Part of the chair hit the floor and a leg broke off. But most of it hit Rodriguez.

He sure looked down for the count.

Ans had feeling in his hands again. Pins and needles feeling, but he could control them. So he picked up Rodriguez's knife.

Jewel was still staring at Rodriguez's fallen form with fury in her eyes. Ans offered her the knife. She shook her head. She still had most of the chair in her hands, and she used it to poke Rodriguez's body.

He didn't move. Apart from breathing.

She tossed the chair aside. She picked up the leg that broke off. Nodded at Ans.

"This suits me better."

Ans made the mistake of nodding. His head swam and he listed one side. Jewel was quick to grab him. Slipped under his left arm, so she could hold him up and he could still hold the knife in his shaky right hand.

"I don't think they're carrying their phones," Jewel said. "They never once pulled one out, and I think I heard Smith complain about it."

"You think they put our phones where their phones are?"

Jewel nodded. "We need to find the others first, though."

"Right," he said. "Bishop's on the third floor. Did you hear them say anything about Faye?"

"No," Jewel said, "but Sorenson's down here somewhere. I'm pretty sure that's because she's down here."

Ans gritted his teeth. "Then let's go get her."

Glorious.

Oh, magnificence.

The feeding. Oh, yes, the feeding would be exquisite. This new kill. This *latest* kill. This second kill in a single night. Not only was this human big. Not only was the human muscled.

Not only did this one lead a merry chase. A brief chase, true, but a chase all the same. Just enough to remind the Eater that He was first and foremost a hunter.

No, this human brought something to the feast better even than those delightful details.

This one had a name for the Eater. A word He didn't know, true, but a name all the same. This one was spiced not only with the terror of the moment, but with sweeter, deeper fears that hearkened back to childhood.

Yes. This was a kill to be *savored*.

The Eater dragged the human carcass back outside to feast under the sky.

Here, He would not be disturbed. The only humans nearby were all within that building. None would witness the feast.

None would know the true danger that stalked them.

At least, not until it was too late.

Oh, yes. Far too late for all of them.

Thus did the Eater once more crouch down to feast under the stars and the waxing moon.

Glorious.

9

When Faye first poked her head out of the room where she'd been imprisoned, she'd seen the bobbing circle of a flashlight's beam farther down the hall.

Without turning on either of the two flashlights she carried, she started down the hall after it. Her left hand trailing along the cool concrete of the wall for comfort in the darkness, while her right kept her chair leg club ready to swing at the first sign of trouble.

And Faye was expecting trouble. It seemed that every nerve in her body was on hyperalert. Every creak of the floorboards. Every change of texture along the wall. Every whiff of dust.

She noticed everything.

Faye was a bundle of nerves as she made her way down that hallway. Her breaths shallow and ragged. Sweat beading on her brow and under her arms. Her heart pounding, pounding, pounding.

She was sure Sorenson — at least, she assumed that was Sorenson ahead of her — was going to turn around and catch her.

Yeah, she had a club, but she'd never been in a fight before.

Plus, every door she passed might have concealed one of Sorenson's gang, ready to pop out at the wrong moment and catch her.

But everything had been quiet since she's heard Sorenson stomp off.

When the light ahead of her moved right and vanished — about where she thought the central staircase was — she paused. Counted to ten under her breath. Then clicked on a beam, pointed it at the floor just before her feet, and worked her way along to that stairwell.

She paused there. Listened.

Nothing.

She couldn't hear any sign of Sorenson on the stairs above her. She had to assume he made no effort at stealth, so he must have hustled up those stairs. He'd probably already gotten where he was going.

Which meant he might be alone with her sweet Bishop *right now*.

Bishop, who wouldn't even be allowed to fight back.

Faye wanted to run up those stairs too. Had to restrain herself. Speed meant noise, and her only advantage would be the element of surprise.

With that in mind, she clicked off her flashlight. Tucked it into her belt beside the other one.

As she thought. The windows at the landings let in plenty of moonlight. Or at least, enough for her eyes to handle, once she gave them a moment to adjust. While she did that, she assessed herself.

Her bottom lip had stopped bleeding, but it still stung from that bastard's slap. And her left shoulder was stiff and achy from the fall.

Fortunately she was right-handed, so she should be able to swing the chair leg just fine, if she ran across Sorenson or any of his cronies. And her boots might not have been sneakers, but the leather was well broken-in, and wouldn't squeak even if she had to run.

She felt silly in the cloak, but was grateful for the warmth as she crept up those dusty stairs as quietly as she could.

Fortunately, the stairs were concrete, not wood. No creaking. She had to be careful though. They were covered in dust and the detritus of a long-closed high school, shut down too quickly for a proper clean-up.

What floor would Sorenson keep Bishop on?

Third. Had to be the third. No way he was going to risk Faye hearing Bishop cry out in pain if one of his boys got heavy-handed.

Sorenson would keep Bishop as far away as possible, so the third floor, at the other end of the hall.

Yes. Faye was certain that was right. The kind of certain she was learning better than to question.

Faye reached the third floor. Got one step into the hallway when she heard Sorenson bellow out her name.

Her stomach tried to drop through the floor and keep going all the way to the center of the earth. Cold fear gripped her. She froze. Positive she'd been spotted. Positive Sorenson had…

No…

No, that *couldn't* be.

She didn't see him. Didn't see any sign of his flashlight. Didn't hear any footsteps speeding towards her.

A moment passed, and no one grabbed her. Caught her. Chased her.

She hadn't been spotted.

A silent, breathless laugh of relief escaped her lips. She put her hand to her speeding heart for a moment and tried to regain control of her breathing.

Once she did, she frowned. Tried to figure out which direction the sound came from.

Farther down the hall. Just where she'd figured they'd stashed her sweet Bishop.

She couldn't risk her flashlight now. Not now. Not when she was so close. Not when Sorenson and one or more of his cronies were so close at hand.

Instead, she poked her head into the hall. Tried to will her pupils to dilate as much as they possibly could.

There was light.

Not much, true, but some moonlight made its way in through some windows at the end of the hall, in the direction she was going.

Enough. She nodded to herself. It was enough light to make sure there was nothing big she could trip over.

Slow step after slow step, Faye eased herself down the hallway, her back to the near wall tightly enough that she could feel the bump of every doorjamb. Poked herself in the side with every doorknob.

But here at the edge of the hall, the floorboards didn't creak. And by keeping her steps slow, Faye made sure each step was safe and silent before she shifted her weight.

Desperate as she was to help her lover, she couldn't risk blowing her rescue now.

Someone screamed, and Faye almost jumped out of her skin.

Her first thought was that the scream was Bishop. That Sorenson was doing something horrible to him *right this second.*

She got as far as setting her jaw and raising her club when she realized no, that couldn't have been Bishop.

The scream had been awful. Heart-wrenching. But it hadn't been close. It certainly hadn't been close enough to have come from a room on this floor.

Faye frowned, not sure what to do.

Was that Ans? Was his need greater?

Was that one of the bad guys? Had Jewel or Ans gotten loose and done a little damage of their own?

No way to know. Only thing she could do was focus on what she knew for sure: Bishop was up here, alone in a room with—

Wait.

Sorenson came stomping out of a room right down by the stairs. His flashlight lit up the path to those stairs and down he went. Swearing the whole way.

This was her chance.

Faye clicked on her flashlight and sped down the hall to that room. That one open door. She held her breath as she reached the doorway and swept her flashlight inside.

There he was. Tied to a chair and down on his left side, like she'd been.

"Bishop!"

"Faye?"

The poor baby sounded weak. Hurt. And he looked like they'd tied him even tighter to the chair than she'd been tied herself.

"I'm here," Faye said, rushing over to him.

She wanted to kiss him. She wanted to take him in her arms. But Sorenson might be back any second, and she had to get him out of that chair.

"On the desk," Bishop said, and his voice sounded strained. "By the headdress. Knife."

Sure enough, there was a pocketknife.

She didn't cut the ropes. She cut the knots. Quick and neat. Whoever owned the knife kept it sharp.

"Thank God," Bishop said, rubbing his wrists.

Then he was standing and neither one of them could wait even a single second longer.

They kissed. A frantic, panicked expression of love that ended all too quickly when she made the mistake of sliding her arms around him and squeezing.

The sound he made was awful.

But he was free, and they were together. They would get out of this yet.

They just had to get to Jewel and Ans.

ANS WASN'T BACK TO NORMAL. NOT BY A LONG SHOT. HE WAS PRETTY damn sure he had a concussion from when Sorenson had slammed his head into the wall. And that punch from Rodriguez *had* wrenched his neck, as well as leaving behind a tender swelling that he was sure was going to bruise.

Not to mention the other aches and pains. In his gut from Rodriguez's earlier punch. His shins and back from his tumble at the staircase. Especially his left shin. Ans really didn't like the way he felt like someone had stuck a hot wire in his shinbone.

No, Ans was not in good shape.

But by the time he and Jewel were halfway down the hall, passing the central staircase, he was at least walking on his own. And the knife in his right hand had stopped shaking.

He didn't want to use it, but it was useless as a threat if he couldn't even hold it.

Still, Jewel had the flashlight they'd taken from Rodriguez in her left hand, and her chair leg club in her right.

Of course, when they'd passed the teacher's lounge, he'd been tempted to stop there. Food. Rest. Oh, those sounded good.

But Bishop and Faye needed them. So stopping wasn't an option.

At least the doors to the lounge were still closed. So Sorenson and his thugs hadn't broken them open.

Ans kept expecting them to run into Smith, but they reached the two open doors at the end of the hall without any sign of him.

Ans and Jewel had been held in a room on the right side of the hallway, so they checked that room first.

Nothing but classroom furniture, some of it broken. And one window broken too. Well, the glass, at least. The chicken wire held firm.

"Had to be where all that noise was earlier," Jewel said.

Ans only gave her a shallow nod in reply.

They turned back to the other room. Crossed the hall. Shined their light inside.

A broken chair. Scraps of cord. But no sign of Faye.

"Good girl," Jewel said. "Got out all on your own."

"She'd head straight for Bishop."

"So that's where we're..." Jewel paused and gave Ans a sharp look. "Baby, are you up to this?"

Ans didn't trust himself to nod. "I am."

"We can get you to the lounge and lock you in."

"No," Ans said firmly. "I'm going to help."

Jewel set her mouth, and Ans could practically hear her think that he wouldn't be much help, if it came to a fight.

"Bishop's my best friend," he said.

Jewel nodded. "Come on then. Central stairs?"

"No," Ans said. "We don't know where Smith is, and the central stairs are closer to reinforcements for him. We take the stairs by the south door."

"Right," Jewel said. "You realize they'll hold Bishop at the other end of the building. So it's not just two flights of stairs, but all the way back down the hall..."

"I'm coming."

"All right."

And together they moved the rest of the way down the hall and turned up the stairs. Jewel was getting impatient, waiting for him, but at least she didn't leave him behind.

Ans couldn't help it. He just couldn't take the stairs very fast right now.

But he did his best.

Blood. Right here in the first floor hallway.

Sorenson clenched his jaw as he went over the smear with the beam of his flashlight. Fresh blood, from the way it glistened. Made the dusty floor tacky, which was how he'd noticed it in the first place. He'd stepped in it as he came off the staircase and his moccasin stuck just enough to notice. Made a disturbing peeling sound as it came up.

Yes. This was definitely a trail of blood.

Not good. He might need to—

Wait.

Maybe it was a trick.

Maybe he missed it earlier. Maybe it was part of whatever York and Magellan were doing to spook their girls and get them going...

Sorenson crouched down on a part of the hardwood that was only dusty, not bloody and not covered in bits of old trash. He braced on the fingertips of his free hand and lowered himself down.

He sniffed, hoping he's smell Karo syrup or something.

But no. It even smelled like blood. Kind of metallic. Didn't people say blood was supposed to taste like copper? Sorenson had never licked a penny, but he'd licked up his share of blood from cuts over the years.

This was blood all right.

Definitely not good.

First Bobby Beef screamed like somebody was laying down a serious hurt on him, and now Sorenson reached the bottom floor to see a trail of blood. Didn't take a genius to figure out that was likely Bobby Beef's blood. Even *York* could have figured that much out.

So who had done this? And where was Bobby?

Answers had to be at the end of the trail of blood.

Well, it was thick here, about three rooms into the hallway, and narrowing as it led down towards...

Wait. That was the near door the trail led to. The *north* door.

But it was the *south* door that he'd found unlocked earlier. The *south* door he and the others had followed York into.

This door — the *north* door — it should have still been locked, just like the front door was.

Or at least, just like the front door had been earlier...

Maybe Sorenson needed to check the front door too. Find out whether or not *it* was still locked.

Later.

Bobby Beef and the trail of blood first.

Well, locked or not, the trail of blood led to the north door. Which meant somebody must have gotten it open. Somebody who wasn't one of his, and wasn't one of York's.

Very not good.

All right. All right. Sorenson needed to keep calm. Letting himself get mad enough to turn the world red, that would have its time and place. Like when he got hold of whoever turned Bobby Beef into a trail of blood.

Right now, though, Sorenson needed to keep cool. Keep smart.

And the cool, smart move was not to go open those doors. No idea who was out there. Or how many, for that matter.

Bobby Beef might not have been the best fighter in his crew, but he was built like a bull. Anybody who could take him down, bleed him out, *and* drag his body away... That was a man worth worrying about.

Sorenson didn't like the way his heart was pounding right now. The way his mouth got dry. Those were good things when he was excited. Amped up. Right now they meant he was scared.

Just another reason to keep his cool. Couldn't let that show or there'd be dissension in the ranks.

All the same. He needed to marshal the troops. Double-quick time.

Sorenson turned and hustled to Staging Room Three, where Cruiser and Grinder were supposed to be keeping Girard and Magellan on ice. And they better be right where he...

Sorenson opened the door, and what he saw made the world start to go red on him.

Grinder, gone.

Girard, gone.

Magellan, gone.

Cruiser, face down on the floor. Unconscious or dead. A broken chair on the floor beside him. Cut ropes over next to another chair a few feet away.

Sorenson held his lips closed tight. His jaw clenched even harder. All the muscles from his abs on up started pulsing with the need to hit something. To break something.

Preferably some*one*.

There was only one good target for him, and that one didn't look very satisfying. There were a few student desks, over against the far wall under the windows, but they weren't close enough to be useful.

And the teacher's desk against the long wall in the back of the room, that was too big to bother with.

The word "LOSER," written on the chalkboard, felt like a personal message to him from Magellan.

"God. Fucking. *Damn it!*"

Sorenson strode into the room, picked up the broken chair, and threw it at the nearest wall.

It finished breaking. Fell in a pile of scrap wood.

It wasn't enough. Not nearly enough.

Tension sang through all his muscles now. He panted for breath. His heart pounded like it was trying to set speed records. The whole world was tinged in red. His fists clenched and unclenched.

All his plans, falling apart.

Faye *denied* him. *Mocked* him.

Someone took down not one, but *two* of his troops. At least one of them dead. Maybe both. The third member of his posse M.I.A.

Cruiser moaned.

Not dead then.

"Get up, you worthless piece of shit," Sorenson said. He kicked Cruiser in the shoulder to flip him over, getting a small moan of pain for his trouble.

Cruiser still had his eyes squeezed shut. His whole face screwed up in pain.

"I said *get up*. Get up or I'll *show* you pain."

"Gimme a sec, asshole," Cruiser said, bringing both hands to his head.

Asshole? *Asshole?*

Sorenson kicked Cruiser in the gut hard enough to double him over. Knocked the wind out of him, too.

He lay there, moaning silently.

"Bobby Beef is down. Probably dead. Won't know for sure until we find his body. Grinder's gone. Magellan and Girard too. And here I find you, on the floor."

Sorenson reached down and slapped Cruiser across the face.

"Now you get up and report, or you'll wish whoever killed Bobby got to you first."

Sorenson crouched there, imagining himself like a tiger ready to pounce. He tapped his fist lightly against his palm.

Faye's derision, that was York's fault. But everything that happened in *here*? That was all on Cruiser. And he had some *'splainin'* to do.

Cruiser swallowed hard, then, with a moan, he started to sit up. One hand on his gut and another on his head.

"You are a serious asshole, Sorenson. I won't forget you kicked me when I was down."

"You fuck, you should be glad I didn't do worse. Now *report.*"

"Yes, fucking, sir." Cruiser threw a mocking salute, then slowly but surely, got to his feet.

"It's like this," he said, wavering on his feet. "We had everything under control. Then we heard a scream of pain, somewhere in the hall. Sounded like a guy. Figured Bishop and Bobby Beef were up on three, and the only guy down here was you."

Sorenson spun his wrist in a get-on-with-it gesture.

"Right, so I figured that meant someone else had to be here. Somebody…"

Cruiser wavered for a moment. Put his hands on his knees. Managed a few deep breaths.

Sorenson let the prick get himself together.

"Somebody," Cruiser continued, "who wasn't ours or York's. Figured that meant we needed to halt the festivities, gather our respective groups, and get the hell out of here."

"*That's* what you figured?" Sorenson shook his head. "Didn't even confirm it first?"

"I sent Grinder out to check it out. But I figured tonight's games were done. So I cut Magellan and Girard loose." He winced in pain. "Bitch hit me with a chair. Twice."

"Serves you right," Sorenson said, shaking his head slowly. "Fuck her and fuck Magellan. Should have left them tied up."

"What the fuck are you thinking, man?" Cruiser said. "I leave them tied up and somebody comes in and *does something* to them, we become accessories. Maybe even to some serious shit beyond anything we've done tonight. Maybe…"

Cruiser frowned, blinked again.

"Did you say Bobby Beef is dead?"

"Come on," Sorenson said, and led Cruiser out into the hallway. Little bitch was moving pretty slow, but Sorenson let it go, just like he let that little tirade go. A leader had to know when to let the troops have their say.

Instead, Sorenson showed him the trail of blood.

That was all it took. Cruiser turned and puked like a pussy.

"Now," Sorenson said, ignoring the puke, "Magellan and Girard, they're probably on their way to Faye..." Sorenson shook his head. "Fuck. Tell me you have your blade?"

Cruiser patted his belt. Shook his head, then winced like shaking his head had been a very bad idea. He leaned against the wall and his breathing got ragged.

"*Fuck,*" Sorenson said. "They're going to cut Faye loose." He grabbed Cruiser by the shoulders. "I'm going straight there. Find Grinder and haul ass up to Bishop's room, because that's where they'll go next."

Cruiser gave the shallowest nod Sorenson had ever seen, but it was enough. He turned and started running down the hall, his flashlight beam bobbing ahead of him.

But he had the feeling he was already too late.

Grinder better be down here somewhere.

JIMMY SMITH HATED BEING CALLED "GRINDER." HE WANTED A COOL nickname. Like "Big Poppa" or "Roller" or "Jimmy Dimes" or something with a little style to it. The kind of nickname a balling rapper would have.

He knew better than to bitch though. Sorenson handed out the nicknames, and *he* thought "Grinder" was a compliment. A statement about how Jimmy wore down other teams on the court.

Yeah. Maybe. But it sounded like everything Jimmy did looked like hard work. But a good baller, he made everything look easy.

Nothing should have *looked* like hard work. So a nickname like "Grinder," Jimmy just couldn't take it as a compliment.

Hell. Even Rodriguez — a shooting guard for Chrissakes — got Cruiser for a nickname. Smooth and stylish.

Nothing Jimmy could do about it though. If he said the wrong thing, Sorenson would tag him with something even worse.

Sorenson was like that.

But you know what? Fuck Sorenson and his stupid "this will win me Conroy back" bullshit. It was a stupid ploy in the first place. And worse than that, it was *boring as fuck*.

Jimmy and Cruiser were just supposed to sit there and watch Magellan and Girard while they were tied to chairs. Just *sit there* and not do anything. Not have any fun, even though Girard had that phat ass and those juicy tits on display in that skintight costume of hers.

Like she *wanted* somebody to be man enough to reach out and grab some. Even if she acted like she didn't.

And Jimmy was *supposed* to just keep his hands to hisself.

What kind of leader didn't throw the troops a little fun?

A bad leader, that's what.

Then there was that fucking scream, and Cruiser, he couldn't go check it out. Oh, no. Maybe he was the one with the "ten years of boxing," but when it came to the risk of a fair fight, he pussed out and made Jimmy go.

Well.

Jimmy saw that smear of blood on the floor. Trailed all the way to that door and out. And what, Cruiser just thought Jimmy was going to kick that door open like some Navy SEAL or some shit?

No way, man.

The blood went one way, so Jimmy went the other. If Cruiser asked, Jimmy would claim he was just checking on Sorenson, in that room at the end of the hall, where he stashed Conroy.

What did he call it? Staging Room One?

But fuck that too.

If Sorenson was in there, he'd rip Jimmy a new one for bothering him. And probably accuse him of something like "abandoning his post."

And if Sorenson *wasn't* in there...

Then Conroy would be in there all on her lonesome...

And there wasn't a hotter piece of ass in school than Faye Conroy.

Jimmy was probably going to catch hell from Sorenson anyway. Might as well have a little fun too...

But that door was open when Jimmy got there. Sorenson was gone and so was Conroy.

That was the exact moment Jimmy decided Sorenson and his whole plan could fuck the hell off. He ducked into the room next door. Grabbed his backpack from the pile on the other side of the oversized teacher's desk.

Why the hell did teachers need such big desks any—

For a second. For *one* second, Jimmy considered snagging the other three backpacks and dropping them off among the trees somewhere.

Naw. Fuck that. Sorenson was going to be pissed enough as it was. Why should Jimmy make his own life more difficult?

He didn't take time to change though. He grabbed his backpack, slung it over one shoulder, and shoved his way out the south side door and into the chilly ass moonlight.

Jesus! Cold as a good glass of Cristal out here. Haunted fucking moon big up above, and bright enough Jimmy didn't need his flashlight as he hustled across the lawn in front of creepy old Colver High, heading for the grove of trees that were all that stood between his half-naked ass and freedom.

Maybe those stoners were stupid enough to still be hanging around? They were wimps, but there were like ... five of them? And Jimmy was only one now, and dressed in nothing but clown makeup and this lame costume loincloth.

Nah. They'd be too spooked to do anything.

Jimmy clicked on his flashlight as he made his way between the trees. Shivering, and not just because of the cold.

No, in the back of his mind he kept thinking about that smear of blood. At least, it sure looked like blood. Smelled like it too.

Who caused that? And just where exactly where *they?*

Second thoughts fluttered in his gut and cold sweat dripped down his face and neck. Maybe he would have been better off back there with Cruiser. Maybe...

Naw.

Couldn't have been blood. Must have been some trick of York's.

And that scream, that was more like a shout, wasn't it? Yeah, maybe it was. Maybe it was just the moment, the way Cruiser and the others reacted, made Jimmy think it sounded worse than it was.

'Cause Sorenson, everyone knew he had a temper. Would have been just like him to come down the hall away from Conroy before he shouted in frustration.

And Magellan and Girard, they'd have said *anything* if it meant getting cut loose.

Yeah, all that made sense to Jimmy as he wove his way through the trees, following the bobbing light of his flashlight beam.

He was tight down below the waist, though. Like deep down he knew that had been a scream, and he knew that someone who wasn't one of theirs had to have caused that scream.

But just in case there was someone around to see how scared he was, Jimmy just played it cool. Pretended he wasn't scared at all. That his heart was only pounding to keep him warm. Stave off the cold. That his sweating was just because he hadn't warmed up before he took this run and...

...and how much farther was the fence anyway?

Wait. There it was. Not more than a dozen yards now, past the edge of the tree line.

Jimmy cut through the last of the trees and threw his backpack over the cyclone fence.

He ran closer.

Grabbed the loose spot. Pulled it wide.

Taloned hands grabbed his shoulders. Their grip ground his shoulder bones painfully. Their talons dug into his flesh until blood trickled from each spot.

"You smell like fear," a grating, harsh voice whispered in his ear. "You smell *delicious.*"

THRILLS.

Shivery delights.

First that oh-so-big and delightful meal. Hefty and strong and fleeing in terror. A meal well worth savoring.

But no sooner did the Eater finish that meal than another presented itself.

Another meal, running. Sweating out aromatic fear.

Oh, how the meal ran across the lawn and through the trees.

Oh, how that foolish little meal did not know he was followed. And yet still, such sweet, sweet fear came wafting off of him while he ran.

The Eater delighted in the scent as He loped in pursuit. Silent as the moonlight. Ominous as a storm front.

Yes. The Eater was sure that even this little running meal sensed Him, somewhere within the primal parts of his nature. The hairs on the back of his neck, perhaps.

For his fear stank all the sweeter in his rush for an outer barrier he would never reach.

The Eater, He followed closer and closer. Gave the meal hope. Let the meal reach the barrier, before clamping down with an unyielding grip.

A rip. A tear. And the feast began.

Sweet, delightful flesh and bone, blood and sinew. Oh, how the Eater gobbled it all down with urgency now. *Need.*

But no sooner did the Eater finish than He felt the gnawing pangs anew, deep within His belly. Pangs that were not *sated* by food, but worsened.

It was the Eater's nature to slake His hunger with such food as He could grasp, only to have His hunger spike all the sharper once the meal was finished.

And this latest meal was finished all too soon.

Three delightful meals in quick succession.

Three *glorious* meals.

But the Eater needed more.

More. More. More. More. More. More. More. More…

Damn it.

Damn it. Damn it. *Damn it!*

Sorenson was hustling up the stairs at the south end of the building. He'd gotten to Faye's room to find her gone. Some cords on the floor. Her chair broken.

He'd broken another chair in frustration. Lost some time stomping around, swearing. Finally, though, he'd slowed his roll enough to check out the situation.

The cords on the floor hadn't been cut. Looked like they'd been gnawed at a bit, in places, but not cut. And he knew that Magellan and Girard had Cruiser's knife, because that pansy ass couldn't even handle those two when they were *tied to chairs.*

All those boxing lessons, and for what? Just so Cruiser could fail to hold onto a wuss and a girl, when they were *tied to fucking chairs.*

Just how much worse was tonight going to get?

At least there was no blood in that room. No sign that Faye had fallen prey to whoever had offed Bobby Beef.

Assuming Bobby Beef *was* dead. Sorenson just couldn't be sure of anything anymore.

Anyway, since the cords weren't cut, that meant it wasn't Magellan and Girard who cut Faye loose. Which meant somehow she'd managed to get *herself* loose.

That one was on Sorenson. *His* bad. Hadn't tied her tight enough. Or maybe he'd just underestimated how athletic she really was.

Weren't the cheerleaders always bitching that they didn't get enough respect as athletes?

Well, after tonight, Sorenson would respect their athleticism more.

But right now, he needed to get to York before Faye did. Because Sorenson had no doubt in the world that she was making a bee line for her boy-toy, and he'd wasted enough time in here already.

By all rights, Faye *should* have been wasting time checking the second floor for her precious York. After all, far as she knew he could have been tucked away in any classroom on any floor. Or a bathroom, for that matter. Any room at all, except for the one York had managed to lock.

But the way this night was going, Sorenson was sure she was headed straight for Bishop as though she'd found a fucking map.

And Sorenson had to get there before she gnawed *him* free too. Because since this whole night was going to hell, before getting out of here Sorenson might as well take the opportunity to lay a serious beat down on York.

Wouldn't hurt Sorenson's chances with Faye any worse at this point. And so far Sorenson hadn't gotten in any kind of real hits since that shot at the dance. Just knocked him over with a shout, and that wasn't very satisfying.

Only Cruiser and Bobby Beef had really gotten to lay any serious smack down on the jerk behind this whole clusterfuck. The one whose fault all this was in the first place.

York.

Yeah, hitting York a few dozen times while Faye begged him to stop would feel *really* good. Not to mention reminding her which of them was the *real* man.

Yeah, she'd deny it out loud, but deep down inside, she'd know the truth. And sooner or later, that truth would come bubbling out of her and she'd come running back to the man she should have been with all along.

John Sorenson.

Besides, just getting a chance to lay some punches into York would feel just fucking *wonderful* right now.

Cathartic. Wasn't that the word?

Then, with York battered and bloody, Sorenson could take off. Hook up with Lisa O'Leary maybe. Work off some of this aggression another way, until Faye came around.

Yeah, York was probably enough of a bitch-ass to run to the principal about tonight. Maybe even the cops. But Sorenson knew he hadn't done anything so bad tonight that his skills on the court — not to mention his daddy's money, which was the only good thing Sorenson ever got from the bastard — couldn't get him out of.

A little fighting. A little horseplay.

Nothing compared to whatever had happened to Bobby Beef.

If that was, in fact, his blood.

Sorenson was on the third floor now, and starting down the hall. He saw the bobbing circle of a flashlight beam ahead of him down the hall.

Had to be Faye. So she hadn't reached York yet.

Good. Very good.

Sorenson killed his beam and slowed down. Felt like an honest-to-God real stalking Indian brave now, with those moccasins on his feet.

Quiet. Stealthy as a fucking green beret.

Yeah.

Sorenson crept down the hall, holding distance, but not closing yet.

Cruiser ought to be up here by now, or at least holding steady over by the stairs. Waiting for his leader, like a good soldier. Maybe with Grinder right beside him.

Yeah, this might work out even better than Sorenson thought...

FAYE WAS NOT A VIOLENT WOMAN BY NATURE, BUT AS SHE LED HER LOVE down the north stairs, even her grip on her flashlight was white-knuckled. To say nothing of her grip on her club.

Frankly, she knew it was better that Bishop had the knife tucked into a pocket of his zoot suit.

Faye was looking for payback.

Tying her to a chair was bad enough. *Slapping* her was *bad enough*. But Bishop needed a hospital. There was no way he didn't have at least three or four broken ribs. And the pounding he'd taken to his poor, sweet belly was *already* showing bruises.

And she worried about this headache of his. He said they hadn't hit him in the head, but they'd still knocked him out...

So as she rounded the landing between the second and first

floors, and saw the bubble of a flashlight coming up the next lowest flight of stairs, she shushed Bishop. She clicked off her flashlight, and they both stepped back to the lower stairs of the next flight up.

She could hear someone talking quietly to himself. Sounded like ... swearing in Spanish.

"Rodriguez," Bishop whispered, and she nodded.

As Rodriguez reached the landing, she swung her club as hard as she could, with both hands.

She caught him in the chest, not the head. Darn it.

Still, it was a solid blow, and he wasn't ready for it. Rodriguez cried out and fell backward, rolling all the way down those concrete steps to the first floor.

Faye was after him like a shot. Bishop hot on her heels, his flashlight lit and trained on their enemy.

Rodriguez reached the ground floor first, and didn't even try to get up. He just lay there, his crossed arms raised to shield his head.

"*No más! No más!*" he said, tears streaming down his face.

Faye raised her club. Bishop grabbed her wrist.

"He's surrendering," Bishop said.

"*Sí!* Yes! I surrender!"

"What have you done with Jewel and Ans?" Faye asked. And Bishop didn't stop her from holding the club in a threatening fashion, though he gave the hall a quick once-over with his flashlight while Rodriguez answered.

"I cut them loose," he said, still holding his arms up like Faye might hit him again. Which she was still considering. "Then your girl hit me with a chair. Twice. They took off while I was out."

"Must be looking for us," Bishop said.

"What about the others?"

"Sorenson said Bobby Beef's dead. Grinder's gone. Probably hightailed it. Sorenson's looking for you guys."

"Where are our phones?"

"Other end of the hall. Right next to the room Sorenson was keeping you, Faye."

"Don't talk to me like we're friends," she said, her voice so cold that Bishop actually looked surprised. "The cops are hearing about *all* this. Believe it."

"Fine," Rodriguez said. "I'll just grab my phone and leave."

"Fuck your phone," she said. "You're not calling for help."

"Fine." Rodriguez scooted back across the floor and crossed something sticky. "Sorenson said this door might be open. Can I use it?"

"Go."

Rodriguez was shaky as he got to his feet. Good. But before he made his way out the door, he turned back to say, "Uh, look. I think there's someone else here. Somebody turned Bobby Beef into a smear of blood."

He pointed to the hallway floor. Bishop lit it up, and it sure did look like blood.

Faye frowned.

"Just thought you should know." Rodriguez turned and went straight out through the door.

As it closed behind him, Bishop said, "That's the wrong door. That door was locked earlier."

An icy, powerful sense of foreboding gripped Faye.

Somewhere outside, Rodriguez screamed.

The Eater turned away from the wet, bloody grass near the outer barrier. His talons clenched and unclenched. Wanting more. Wanting another bite.

But this latest meal was already done.

Too fast. He'd eaten too fast. Forgotten to *savor* the meal. The heady aroma of fear had been too much to resist.

But now that meal was gone. Flesh and bone, blood and sinew, all eaten. Devoured.

Finished.

More. There had to be more.

Somewhere nearby, there had to be more.

Yes. The Eater could sense them. Feel them. Humans, back inside the building. Humans who did not yet know that their lives were over. That they only counted their precious seconds until they met their glorious fates as the most recent devoured by the Eater.

A noble fate. They should thank whatever gods would listen to them.

The Eater smiled.

He loped back through the grove of live trees, toward the building. Toward His next meals. Toward...

What was this?

Another meal, leaving the building even now?

Yessssss.

And this one stank not of mere fear, but *terror*. Heady, wonderful terror. Yes. This one was wounded. Hobbling. Panting. A mess.

The Eater pounced.

Another glorious meal.

And once He finished with this one, there were still others nearby...

10

OCTOBER 31ST, 12:01 AM.

That scream on the other side of the door. That could only have been Rodriguez.

And there was a freaking *blood trail* on the floor.

That was the limit, far as Bishop was concerned. And Faye, she must have been on the same page, because he looked at her, she looked at him, and they nodded.

They turned and ran down the hall, away from the scream.

Oh, how running hurt.

Every step was torture. A wave of pain through his rib cage. Every attempt at breath made it worse. Bishop knew he definitely had broken ribs now, because he felt as though they were poking around, damaging his insides as he took each stride.

Plus, he was running in slow motion. Hardly even anything that could be called a run. More like a slow jog.

Faye was keeping back with him. As though she were afraid that if she pulled away, she might never see him again.

And maybe she wouldn't. Something bad was going down here tonight. Something much worse than Sorenson and his thugs.

Something that made trails of blood, and generated screams that sure as hell *sounded* fatal.

The dust in the air made him want to cough. Bishop had to force his breaths in and out through his mouth. Through his gritted teeth. Because trying to breathe through his nose was even worse.

His legs felt like lead. This was stupid. He was holding her back.

"Go," he rasped at Faye. "You go … I'll … catch—"

"No, you will not. I'm not leaving you, Bishop York. Not ever again."

He couldn't see her face, with her running next to him through the dark hallway. Not really. All he could really see clearly was the bouncing circle of light from his flashlight beam.

But he knew her expression all the same. He'd seen the determined flash of her eyes many times. The firm way her jaw was set. He could hear both those things in her voice.

Yeah, she wasn't going to do the smart thing and save herself.

Wait. Save…

"Ans," he panted. "Jewel."

"Already ahead of you," she said. "Soon as we reach the stairs. Voice'll carry better there."

Bishop nodded and kept his feet moving as fast as he could. And honestly, it was taking all his concentration to do that. The pain through his ribs, emphasized even more by his bruised and battered core muscles, it was almost too much to bear. Kept his heart pounding like he was sprinting flat out, and his poor zoot suit was sopping now, with his sweat.

But damn it, he was *not* going to make Faye carry him. Or drag him. Or whatever.

Because he was sure she'd do it if he stopped running.

They reached the central staircase, and Faye skidded to a stop. Bishop tried to stop with her, but she shoved him ahead.

He couldn't help the grunt of pain when she shoved him. Wasn't as though he could stop the sound.

So he turned and kept moving. She'd catch up any second anyway. She could outrun him in a sprint any day of the week even under good conditions. Though, normally, he could lose her in a long distance run without a sweat.

Long distance, that was what Bishop was best at. Running 'round and 'round a track, or down the streets and up and down the hills of Long Pine City. Didn't advertise that he did it, but he did it five times a week all the same.

Sprinting, he was never any good at. Especially now, when most of his body felt like it was falling apart.

But he had to run. Had to get away. Or else Faye *would* try to carry him. And then whoever was back there would catch both of them.

Bishop couldn't let that happen.

He heard her behind him, bellowing up those stairs in her best cheerleading tones. Her voice echoed out off of the concrete walls all around him.

"RED EIGHT! RED EIGHT! RED EIGHT!"

That made absolutely no sense to Bishop. But he trusted that she knew what she was doing. He kept moving.

And sure enough, she caught him up before he'd gone two rooms farther. Striding smooth and easy right beside him.

"What..." he started, but she didn't wait for the whole question.

"Cheerleading thing, for whenever we're away from our home court," she said, apparently not needing even a little effort to keep up with him right now. "Red is our danger code, and eight means the exit's the way we came in."

"Why—"

"Baby, it's a dangerous world out there. When a bunch of hot teenage girls go places in a group, they need to be organized."

Smart. Bishop couldn't help smiling. Yeah, the code wouldn't mean anything to Ans, but from what Nagy said earlier, Ans and Jewel were being held together. No reason to think they'd been separated.

Maybe they were all going to get out of this yet.

They were maybe three rooms from the south door when they heard an echoing shout in return.

"Faye! Bishop! You go! We'll be along in a sec!"

The echoes stole some of the details of the voice. Bishop thought he knew who that was, but he had to ask.

"Was ... that..."

"Jewel, yes." Bishop could hear the frown in her voice as she continued. "Hope they get a move on."

Bishop was going to say something that might inspire confidence. But in that moment he heard the door at the north end blast open. Shattered inwards.

And a laugh chased him down the hall. A low, long, menacing laugh.

Bishop tried harder for speed, and hoped that Ans and Jewel really would be along any second. Maybe even coming down the south stairs...

ANS AND JEWEL WERE JUST ABOUT ONE ROOM PAST THE CENTRAL staircase on the third floor when they heard the echoing shout.

"RED EIGHT! RED EIGHT! RED EIGHT!"

"Was that Faye?" Ans asked.

"Yep," Jewel said. "She must have Bishop. Time to go."

"Are you sure?"

Jewel turned a no-shit expression on him, and all Ans could do was nod.

Together they turned to start for the nearest stairs.

"Just where do you two think you're going?"

That was Sorenson's voice, wasn't it? Right ahead of them, like he'd been following.

Then a flashlight clicked on. The light shone straight up across the face of John Sorenson.

"Look," Ans said, "whatever you were trying to do tonight, it didn't work. It's over. And we're all in danger now. There's someone else here."

"I know there's someone else here," Sorenson said, nodding his head, but keeping that light across his face at that spooky angle.

"Pretty sure whoever it is killed Bobby Beef. Maybe Grinder too. Hell, I think I heard another scream a minute or two ago. So maybe Cruiser's dead too."

He actually shrugged. Like maybe he just didn't care anymore.

"Did you hear another scream?" Ans whispered to Jewel.

"Yeah, but it didn't sound like Faye or Bish, so..."

"Let's just get out of here," Ans said, louder, "before whoever scared Faye gets us too."

"You two," Sorenson said, shaking his head. "You aren't going anywhere."

"I've got a club here that says we are," Jewel said. "Ask your boy Rodriguez how hard I hit with it."

"And I've got a knife," Ans said, wishing his voice sounded steadier as he said it. "It doesn't have to come to this."

"Oh, I think it does." Sorenson's smile got even wider. "And when I'm done with you two, I'm going to get some revenge for my boys."

"Faye! Bishop!" Jewel yelled, and her yell was so loud that Ans' ears buzzed. "You go! We'll be along in a sec!"

Sorenson snorted. "I told you. You aren't going anywhere."

"Bring it," Jewel said with a sneer, "you *stupid, useless* piece of pathetic white trash."

That must have been the wrong thing to say to John Sorenson.

"White trash? *White trash?* Bitch, I'll show you white trash."

He pulled a pocketknife of his own now. Flicked it open.

"Fuck," Ans muttered. Of course this dick carried a bigger knife than his friends. He was just that type. The knife Ans got from Rodriguez had a blade only about four inches long, but the one in Sorenson's hands had to be six inches, easy.

A shattering sound from somewhere downstairs. Something heavy and wooden, just ... *demolished.*

A long, low, menacing laugh drifted up the stairs and through the hallway, its echoes playing hell off the concrete walls.

If Sorenson was right about his friends being dead, that laugh had to have come from their murderer.

Lovely. Just what this night needed.

But there was no time to worry about that right now.

Jewel stepped to Sorenson's left, so Ans moved to his right.

Ans hit the bastard in the face with a flashlight beam, but all he did was squint. Must have been ready for it.

And Sorenson, that arrogant prick, he was smiling.

"I'll bleed you both," Sorenson said. "I'll—"

Ans threw his knife at him.

The way Ans had pictured it, the knife was supposed to spin elegantly and then plunge into Sorenson somewhere important. Not fatal, but enough to take him down so they could escape this slaughterhouse. Thigh, maybe. Or shoulder.

The reality, alas, didn't live up to the image.

The knife spun in the air, yeah, but the blade was facing sideways when it hit its target. Bounced off Sorenson's chest. Maybe not even hard enough to leave a mark.

But it sure got his attention.

Sorenson turned to Ans, murder in his eyes. Slashed out with the knife.

Ans jerked backwards. His hurt shin gave out. Down he went on the hardwood floor. All of his bumps and bruises ringing out their own reminders of just how badly he'd been hurt tonight.

But he avoided the blade.

And Jewel took advantage of the distraction.

She swung that chair leg low, in both hands, and cracked Sorenson on the side of the knee.

Sorenson bellowed and went down. Dropped his knife and grabbed his knee with both hands.

"Come on!" Jewel grabbed Ans by the wrist and yanked him to his feet. She still had that chair leg in her free hand.

Together they got moving down the stairs as fast as they could. And Ans had so much adrenaline going now that he was moving at a pretty good clip. Even if his head was swimming and he bounced off a landing wall as he came around.

Worse, he could hear Sorenson behind him. Yelling threats and obscenities.

And following. Already Ans could see the glare of Sorenson's flashlight as he chased after them.

"Faster, baby," Jewel pleaded. "I know you're hurt but you need to *move*."

"Trying," Ans panted, open-mouthed. He could taste bile. Suspected another round of vomit wasn't far off. It was all he could do to keep his feet moving down those stairs without falling. The whole world kept trying to spin, then clicking back into place.

And then Jewel stopped. Let him pass.

"Take *this*!" She yelled, and Ans heard her chair leg bounce off concrete.

But before he could ask, she was beside him again, empty-handed, and holding him up as they hustled down the stairs.

If she threw her chair leg, though, she must have missed. Ans could hear Sorenson getting closer.

"I'm gonna rape you for this, bitch! I'll make your boy watch! Then I'll make *you* watch while I beat him to *death!* Hell. Maybe I'll rape *him* with that fucking chair leg!"

These were the sorts of things Sorenson was hollering nonstop.

And even with the hurt knee he was gaining on them.

By the time Ans and Jewel finally came around the final turn of the staircase and onto the first floor, Sorenson was *too* close.

Sorenson jumped those last few steps. Tackled Jewel to the floor, knocking Ans down in passing.

Ans couldn't help it. He turned his head and vomited bile...

...on the feet of a Thing.

His eyes and his flashlight tracked upward, giving him all too full a view of a thing that looked as though it had come out of a campfire tale. Or maybe some old story about werewolves or manitous or something.

It was taller than a man. Thinner too. With claws and fangs and glowing eyes, and...

...a smile as it licked its chops.

It reached for Ans.

He rolled away.

It laughed again, that haunting laugh.

"There is no escaping the Eater," it said, with a rasping, hellish voice.

Jewel and Sorenson must have heard that, because as Ans came to his feet, they'd stopped fighting. Both were still on the dusty hardwood floor of the hallway, Sorenson still on top of her.

Jewel used the distraction first. Managed to get both feet between herself and Sorenson. Kicked out *hard*. Launched him right at the Thing.

The Thing caught Sorenson and ripped him right in half. Hot blood and gore sprayed out, coating Ans. Coating Jewel. Coating everything.

Ans grabbed Jewel's hand. Yanked her to her feet with a squeal of his own pain.

And they were running again. Slipping and sliding on blood for the first few steps, but still they pushed on.

Everything that Ans was, he dedicated in that moment to escape. Whatever part of him remained from his cave-dwelling ancestors recognized that *this* was the Thing in the darkness that they feared.

And that fear overrode even his pains in his efforts to get away.

For maybe ten steps he actually kept up with Jewel.

But it turned out that the sharp pain Ans had been feeling in his shin — the result of that spill across the concrete stairs earlier — that *had* been a fracture of some kind. And it had taken all the abuse it was going to take.

Because that leg gave out on him.

Ans tumbled to the floor.

Jewel skidded to a stop. Turned to help him.

"Go!" he ordered. One quick flash of his light showed that the Thing back there was already finished with Sorenson and coming after them. "Get away!"

But Jewel grabbed Ans' arms. Helped him up. Helped him run.

But the Thing was getting closer.

"Leave me," he rasped.

"We can make it," she said, terror and determination fighting in her voice.

They reached the south door.

And then the Thing reached them.

GETTING OUT THOSE SOUTH DOORS FELT LIKE AN ACCOMPLISHMENT TO Bishop. He flung them open with both hands, Faye one step behind him.

The moonlight on Bishop's face was a blessing. He could see again, without the aid of a flashlight. Clicked off the beam and stuffed the flashlight into his pocket without even thinking.

The air was chilly, but at least it was dust free. Smelled of pine and fresh grass. And breathing sure was easier on his poor, sore ribs when he didn't have to fight not to cough.

Of course, that was really just a matter of degree. His ribs still flared bits of pain with each breath.

All the same, he hustled down the handful of stairs to the concrete walkway, Faye at his side, a worried expression on her face.

"You think we should go back for them?" Bishop asked.

"I have to get you to safety," she said. Softer, as to herself, she finished. "My fault. This is all my fault. I knew we should have left."

"Don't blame yourself," Bishop said firmly, hating the undercurrent of pain in his voice as he turned east to head for the vast front lawn, then grove of trees and the street.

God! Did he even have his...

Yes. They'd actually left him his keys. They were still in his pocket where they were supposed to be.

Apparently even John Sorenson wouldn't fuck with another man's ride.

But Faye steered Bishop away from that direction. Instead of going east, she was trying to get him to go west. That would lead across the smaller section of lawn, then past the small, boxy gymnasium. Yes, it was a shorter path to the street, but there was no opening there.

And it was the wrong direction.

"The car's that—" He tried, but she cut him off, a spooky look in her eyes and that worried set to her mouth.

"Trust me," she said, and he did.

Bishop moved as quickly as he could across the grass. Faster now, than he had inside. Adrenaline had kicked in. Moved the pain in his chest and stomach into the background.

He wasn't exactly pressing Faye for speed, but he didn't feel as though she could have literally run rings around him as they went.

Fortunately, being stuck at a slower pace meant that the dew on the thick grass didn't start his loafers slipping and sliding. He actually kept his feet under himself, and began to build a steady, rhythmic pace.

It was Faye who almost stumbled, crying out in dismay as they started to pass the gymnasium.

"*No!*"

"What?" Bishop said, slowing to turn and see her instead of trying to take a tight corner.

Tears flooded her eyes. Her lips quivered. But she shook her head. Pushed his shoulder.

"Run!" she said.

"But—"

"*Now!*" She grabbed his wrist and started yanking him along. That set off a fresh round of pain and Bishop hated the whimper that came out of him.

But he got moving again. Faster now. No choice. Not with Faye dragging him.

"Hurry," she said, but tears flowed freely down her face. And her breath came in sniffles. "It *can't* get us too."

"What can't?"

Bishop heard the south doors slam open. A roar split the night air. The roar of a hunter.

He couldn't help glancing back. And what he saw made him run even faster.

Abject terror spilled a whole fresh round of adrenaline through his system. He was barely aware of his pain now as he kicked his speed up a notch. Finally making Faye work to keep up with him.

"Faster," Faye panted. "Faster, bae."

Bishop tried, but he didn't have much more speed.

They were getting close now. To the smattering of old cherry trees that lined this side of the schoolyard, but more importantly, close to the cyclone fence.

Only maybe another twenty strides...

...and there was someone standing there?

The person was in shadow. Bishop couldn't see any details. But the person didn't look big. Shortish. Slight. And watching them?

A second hunting howl sounded behind them. Closer. Impossibly closer.

Sure enough, a glance confirmed that that reject from a werewolf movie was already reaching the gymnasium.

Ten strides to the fence now. Faye, speeding ahead at last.

"No escape," a raspy voice taunted from behind Bishop. "No escape from the Eater."

Hands found his shoulders. A grip tight enough Bishop thought his bones might grind to powder. The squeeze flared sudden awareness of Bishop's damaged ribs once more.

Talons dug into his flesh...

Herbed, scented water drenched Bishop from the front. Enough that some of them must also have splashed the Thing that held him.

Harsh, clear syllables rang out in the night. Like the voice of an angel, speaking some lost language out of the Bible.

The Thing gripping Bishop's shoulders cried out in pain. A sound so loud and sharp the world went quiet.

Bishop could hear only a faint, ringing sound. Not even the frantic beating of his own heart. Those talons gripping his shoulders were gone now, and Bishop thought they might have been the only things holding him upright.

He swayed on his feet. Panting for breath. His legs shook. His ribs, a constant air raid siren of pain. Sweat stung his eyes. Plastered his zoot suit to his body. His hands went to his knees.

But then Faye was there, taking his hands. Helping Bishop take slow, stumbling steps without falling. Leading Bishop to the fence.

Not just to the fence, but to a fresh hole cut in the fence.

Faye pushed him out through that hole, before following herself.

An old woman was standing there, wearing a brightly colored shawl covered in Celtic knotwork over a simple, but warm-looking dress. She had thick, steel-gray hair tied in knots that went all the way to her thin waist. Her expression was fearsome.

She didn't look as though she weighed a hundred pounds soaking wet. But she also looked as though she stood a hundred feet tall. And Bishop couldn't understand that.

She looked vaguely familiar too, but Bishop couldn't place her.

Then Faye was holding him. Tenderly. Gently. But enough that he could feel her arms around him. He returned the favor, while she buried her face in his neck and wept.

Slowly, sound returned to Bishop's world.

The sound of his heart and breathing first, then Faye's weeping, and finally the old woman's words…

No. The old woman's chant.

So it had been the old woman, chanting in that strange, harsh language.

"Well," the old woman said at long last, "you listened when it mattered most. *And* you heard the touch of my thoughts, calling you this way. That's not nothing."

"But Jewel," Faye said, not lifting her face from his neck, but still directing her words at the old woman. "Ans. I … I felt it when they—"

"Aye, they are a terrible loss, and there's no denying it. But don't you go blaming yourself for that, Faye Conroy."

"But Nanna—"

"None of your 'but Nanna's' neither. There'll be things you can see and not help, and there'll be things you can see and prevent. Not always easy to know one from 'tother."

Bishop felt as though he'd come into this conversation quite late, and with the shaky drag of spent adrenaline making him feel slower than normal, he wasn't sure he understood anything Faye and Nanna Conroy were saying.

But one key fact came together in his head.

"Ans," he moaned. "Jewel. They're dead, aren't they?"

Faye started crying again.

"I'm sorry to say it," Nanna Conroy said, "but if they were between you and the Eater, they're dead."

"What was that thing?"

"Is," Nanna Conroy corrected him. "I made it smart quite a bit, to be sure, but nothing I've ever heard of can give the Eater more than a black eye."

"But what—"

"I heard your question, Bishop York. All you need to know is that it's old and it's dangerous and this is where it must be kept."

Nanna Conroy frowned and shook her head.

"Have to gather the girls tomorrow when the sun is shining. Come back and reset those wards. Maybe a little stronger this time..."

"Wards?" Bishop asked. Faye gave him a warning squeeze, but too late.

"Never you mind about wards. You get my granddaughter home and yourself to hospital."

"I'm going with him," Faye said, pulling away from Bishop to give her grandmother a steely glare. "He's in no shape to drive, and I'm not losing him too."

The two women exchanged glares.

"Call your mother then," Nanna Conroy said finally. "She'll be worried sick."

"My phone's in there," Faye said, pointing back to the building Bishop wished they'd never entered. "Bishop's too."

Nanna Conroy frowned. "Fine then. I'll call her. And yes, I'll be getting those phones for you tomorrow. But be off with you now. I have work to do before I leave."

Faye took Bishop's hand, and together they trudged the long walk to his car.

Pain.

Roiling, burning pain.

So long it had been. So very long since anything had last hurt the Eater. He had forgotten that He *could* be hurt.

How?

Who could have that knowledge in this era?

The Eater was certain that nothing had caused Him such pain since ... yes. Since the natives and their shamans had dwelled nearby.

But someone knew.

And that someone knew that the inner boundaries were down, even if the outer bindings remained in place.

That someone knew about those delightful spills of blood.

That someone would know soon about the delicious meals the Eater had enjoyed this night.

Oh!

Oh, if only that someone would wait for the Eater to heal, before returning.

Oh, that would be a feast for the ages.

But no.

The Eater knew better.

Those who had the knowledge, they were never fools. They were careful.

No. The someone who knew, that someone would return tomorrow, while the Eater remained yet crippled and hiding here in this block of cement underneath the building.

That someone would return and refresh the inner binding. Perhaps fortify the outer as well.

Perhaps even add a third.

There was precedent.

But these things, they did not matter. Not really.

Yes, they were angering. Frustrating.

Yes, the Eater wanted to pounce upon all with such knowledge and consume them. Remove them as threats once and for all.

But all bindings had weaknesses. It was their nature, every bit as much as it was the Eater's nature to gorge on all who crossed His path.

All save those two who escaped this night.

The first ever to escape Him.

Well, all bindings had weaknesses.

All bindings eventually frayed and came apart.

Then the Eater would hunt. Kill. Eat once more.

And if those two yet lived, they would be the most delicious, the most *satisfying* meals He ever ate.

Yes.

The Eater had only to wait.

For bindings were not eternal...

...but the Eater was.

SIGN UP FOR STEFON'S NEWSLETTER

Stefon loves to keep in touch with his readers, and loves to keep you reading. The best way for him to do both is for you to sign up for his newsletter.

Sign up at http://www.stefonmears.com/join

If you sign up for Stefon's newsletter, you get...

- Monthly updates about his publishing and travel schedules
- His latest news, in brief, and answers to reader questions
- A free short story for signing up
- List-only offers and occasional specials
- Plus a free short story every month!

ABOUT THE AUTHOR

Stefon Mears knows all the haunted places in his hometown. Stefon has more than twenty-five books to his credit, and he never stops writing. He earned his M.F.A. in Creative Writing from N.I.L.A., and his B.A. in Religious Studies (double emphasis in Ritual and Mythology) from U.C. Berkeley. He's a lifelong gamer and fantasy fan. Stefon lives in Portland, Oregon, with his wife and three cats.

Look for Stefon online:
www.stefonmears.com
himself@stefonmears.com